~Call of the Dove~

By,
Jim Wade Smith

~~~

Cover Design:
Lara Martin

Cover Photo provided royalty free via:
https://pixabay.com/

Photographs of Jim Wade Smith by Lara S. Martin

~~~

CONTENTS

~~~

The Deed   *1*

My Arrival   *2*

Sam Dawkins   *3*

Mars Lucas Claibourne   *4*

Teresa   *5*

Post War Columbia   *6*

The Business Woman   *7*

Between the Glade and the Ball   *8*

Matter of Decency and the Code   *9*

Searching   *10*

Ghosts or Reality   *11*

Discovering Truth!   *12*

Of Shadows and Horses   *13*

Revenge Revelation   *14*

Vengeful Exploration   *15*

The Secret   *16*

Suspicions   *17*

Salvation   *18*

~~~

This book is dedicated to my daughter Lara,
without whose help I could not have completed it. She is truly a Southern
Bell, and a heroine.

~~~

1
~The Deed~

"Father!" I watched in shock and breathless fear as his face turned blue. Only a moment ago, he had been laughing. Then he swayed, and fell directly forward into the dining table. Wine glasses shattered, their stems making little, 'Pops' of sound. Someone screamed. It wasn't me. I was mesmerized with terror. Then, cold dread gave way to hysterical action. I lunged forward and began to pull vainly at his heavy form.

"Daddy!" the more childish name burst from my lips again and again. Many arms pulled me away despite my herculean efforts to reach my father.

Some of the male guests lifted him from the table and lowered him gently to the floor. My younger brother, Franklin was among them, his face ashen.

"Dad, Sir!" he pleaded with his father.

Someone get the doctor! He's in the Library!" Being held firmly, until the doctor arrived, I heard the words,

"Massive heart attack"... "He's gone!"

I tore myself from the clutching hands and rushed to my father. I called his name and kissed the poor closed eyes.

"Daddy, Please, oh God, please..." Franklin looked at me with tears in his eyes while I kept repeating, "Don't go daddy, please don't. Leave me alone! Please don't...Oh God, come ba-a-ck!"

People tried to pull me away, only to recoil in

amazement at the fire in my eyes.

"No, don't you dare! You're trying to take my daddy away! I'll kill you, get away!" The doctor ushered the guests from the room.

"You'll have to forgive Miss Rhyman, she's beside herself with grief, you know. She and her father was very close, poor girl. Quite tragic, oh yes, quite tragic."

A while later, I remember Franklin stroking my hair and pleading,

"Please sis, please, I need your help! I need you to help me! We have to look after dad now. Do you understand me? We have to let the doctor clean him up. C'mon, Kel, you have to get up!"

His pleading finally reached me. I slowly rose and numbly walked away with him. My world was destroyed.

"Dad...Gone!" The thought was numbing. Then, I began to cry while Franklin held me.

The next few days were an endless ordeal of funeral arrangements, financial decisions, and heartbreak. Father had been a very successful businessman. He owned a shipping company called Rhyman and Sons, a company dealing in both land and sea freight. He held the controlling interest in both railroad and ocean vessels. Some called him Rhyman, the railroad magnate. He drove hard, common sense, business deals, and his word was his bond. During the war, his freight cars carried supplies for the government. Later, my two elder brothers rode these same trains to their deaths after joining the "Maryland Contingent of Federal troops."

John Jacob Rhyman kept his very substantial fortune in his own bank. Now, only Franklin and I were left in the family. Ironically, father's head for business was prevalent in me, while Franklin was his mother's son, delicate and fun loving. He loved the ladies, one in particular. My brother is the last chance for the Rhyman name to continue. I, on the other hand, had never shown much interest in the opposite sex, preferring to be my father's shadow. I learned much from him that would stand for my benefit later.

Father's will was read by his lawyers. Everything was left to Franklin and me jointly but, to my surprise, with the stipulation that my approval was required for all decisions made by the boards of the various companies. Franklin seemed relieved, apparently content to bask in his carefree lifestyle. He gave me no problem until the day father's accountant made inquiry of me about a recent acquisition of property.

"What is it worth, Miss Rhyman?" the accountant asked.

"I have to know, uh for the books." He apologetically gestured with his hands. There on the desk was a descriptive deed of a plantation on a large section of land with buildings marked, '*Claibourne Manor*'.

"I'll go and see", was my immediate decision. For the first time, Franklin argued with me.

"Listen sis, the war's only been over for a year and six months, you can't be serious. You are a Yankee, and Yankee's aren't looked on with favor down south, now. This place is in South Carolina, the place that fired the first shot against Fort Sumter! It's probably just and old eye sore, anyway. Why don't you sell it sight unseen?" He growled.

"I need a vacation." I argued. "And I can take care of myself! However, I'll compromise with you. You can go too if you want."

"I can't, but if I can talk you out of it, I'll follow later." He sighed.

"I'll be careful." I reassured him.

"You had better be." Franklin grumbled.

"Good!" I triumphantly replied, "I'll go in mid-summer!"

A few, months later, I was heading south toward the property my father owned unprepared for all the feelings that would nag at me. I was by myself and lonely. The train whistle sounded mournful as it echoed through the mountain passes of Virginia. As the scenery quickly raced by outside my train window, I couldn't fight back the memories of my father and the feeling I was leaving him behind. The ride was long and depressing. Thoughts of how much I loved him ran through my mind. I was devastated by his death. I had won the property in one of his beloved Saturday night poker games.

The last owner of the place was one, Samuel Dawkins. He had lost heavily, then, put the property up to try to recoup his losses. Father claimed the deed. Mr. Dawkins had to be forcefully ejected when he threatened to pull a gun. Careful scrutiny of the papers had disclosed that Mr. Dawkins had received the property from a certain Colonel Jasper Calhoun Claibourne. Sam Dawkins had been the former overseer for the plantation. Colonel Claibourne was the third in of rich plantation owners. The estate was established in his forebears name by the King of England in 1756.

2
~My Arrival~

'*The trees*,' the trees were great, gnarled, specters of oak supporting a green, rustling, canopy that moved and swayed in the warm summer breeze! They formed a square, even pattern around the old, handmade brick and whitewashed structure known locally as, '*Claibourne Manor*'.

The two largest of the trees centered and framed the entrance to the colonnaded mansion. They were at least six feet through at their bases, and they rose towering into the blue southern sky. Their loftiness took my breath away, and I gasped at the thought of being one of the little yellow birds now flitting and singing among the branches.

I vaguely heard the driver when he clucked at the horses. He had seemed a dirty unkempt sort. I also certainly had my doubts about committing myself to the rickety old coach. '*But the horses*,' the horses were a perfectly matched pair of bays! Father and I loved horses, and he had taught me to ride. They were very intelligent creatures. If you were lucky enough to have one love you, only death could destroy the loyalty given. '*How could a low sort of person have come by such beautiful animals*?' I wondered...

Looking at those horses made me remember a certain horse kept at our stables in Baltimore. Everyone said that he was an outlaw, and he certainly had proven them right day by day. I thought the stallion was grand. I even refused to have him gelded, much to my father's ire. I tried constantly to gentle the horse, but failed miserably.

Then one day after a particularly bad session with him a voice behind me had drawled,

"Pahdon me, Miss Rhyman, ma'am. This hoa'se done gone an' turned yo' down. He's what's known as ah' one man hoa'se. When he loves, he's goin' ta go all the way, holdin nothin' back. He's not goan to take any less from his mastuh, eithah. He's got ta respect whoevah he chooses foa his mastuh. An' he can't respect anyone who is afraid of him."

I whirled in anger. "Oh is that so? And I suppose you know what he's thinking, too! Did you just have a little talk with him, or maybe you can read horse's minds? By the way, what are you doing in my stable?"

I stared cooly at the young man dressed in a lace-ruffled shirt with puffed sleeves. The shirt was open at the throat, revealing bronze skin. His hair was a light, golden brown, and a wisp of it curled over one eyebrow. Black leather sleeve garters matched the large buckled belt and polished boots. His even, white teeth flashed in a smile, which was strangely disturbing to me.

I felt undressed, naked. All the men that I had ever met had been simpering, bowing pipsqueaks compared to my father. For the first time I felt bewildered and out of control.

"Well sir," I demanded, "Are you a trespasser, or what?" The man infuriated me even farther by casually turning away toward the stallion's stall door.

"Yes", came the answer, "and no!"

"What do you mean, sir?"

"Yes ta' yoah' fust three questions, ma'am, an' no to the last."

"Then state your business, sir!" I shot back. Another pause,

"Ah'm lookin' foah a hoase."

6

He turned to me. That disturbing smile flashed again,

"One bettah than average, Miss. Rhyman." Another pause,

"Mah be this one heah." He turned and looked at me with black eyes that challenged.

'*Well, sir, whoever you are,*' I gleefully told myself. '*If it's a challenge that you want, then I'll give you one!*'

"Oh, so then maybe this one, you say, did you not, sir? He's unbroken you know, but he will not be cheap! However, I shall be pleased to make a deal with you if you so desire, or, should I say dire? If you conquer the horse, I will give him to you. If you do not, sir, you will pay me double my price."

My father could have done no better at driving a harder deal. I knew the stallion, and there was no way this man could handle him.

"Well do we have a deal?" I asked sweetly.

The answer came so swiftly I was taken aback.

"Yo'all most definitely have a deal, ma'am! You've lost yo'self a hoase!"

Immediately the stall latch was thrown, and the stranger stepped inside! The stallions scream brought me to my senses. Inexcusable! I had allowed my temper to endanger the young man's life! I rushed to the stall door intending to order the man out before Pharaoh crushed him into the floor of his stall. It was too late. The man fearlessly stood in the center of the stall, while the stallion reared above him! Pharaoh's hooves flailed only inches from his face! The dark eyes of the young man were unflinching, and he smiled! He smiled, while Pharaoh came back down to earth before him, stamping and pawing. The horse's eye's rolled. They burned with a devilish light that sparked and danced like flame.

I tore my eyes away to see the stranger kneeling in the

straw. He reached down and calmly grasped some of the feed hay. He did not look up as Pharaoh charged again. He came low with his ears laid back and his huge yellow teeth bared. In the split second, before the horse would have been upon him, the man looked up at Pharaoh. He was still smiling, but *'those eyes*!' They danced and sparked with the same light that I had observed in the eyes of the stallion! Pharaoh world away and stood pawing and tossing his head. The black eyes of the stranger never left the eyes of the horse. He slowly stood up.

A whicker, exactly like that of a horse came from the stranger as he stepped one step forward and offered the hay. The stallion's ears came forward curiously. He stared, but the killing light was gone. Then, with one hesitant step and a toss of the head, Pharaoh came! He stopped short, and stretched forth his neck. Not for the hay but to sniff the face of the young man. While he was sniffing, the man softly blew his breath into the flared nostrils. Gradually, the horse's trembling body stilled. With a low, rumbling neigh, Pharaoh took the hay from the hand of the stranger!

"You still have to ride him!" I jealously watched the man stroke Pharaoh's neck.

"Do yo'all doubt that ah' can?" He smiled that infuriating smile again. I watched him step away from the horse. With a low nicker Pharaoh followed!

"Could ah trouble yo'all foah ah lead rope, please ma'am? Ah shall have to take Pharaoh, ah believe that is what yo'ah fath'uh called him, outside to mah' carriage. He is Arab isn't he? Yo'all has theh' papah's of coahse?"

'*Of course!*' I was beaten and tricked! Apparently my father and this man had conspired in some way! I turned in anger at my failure. Disgusted, I replied,

"I'll get the rope."

I had never seen that gentleman again. A pang of grief filled my heart as I thought of my father. He had surely conspired to save his daughter from injury. But this was before the war, I mused, looking again to the old mansion before me. I sat mesmerized, awestricken at the dilapidation. Yet, there was still a grandeur that whispered through the apparent neglect. The ivy-covered columns had probably been white, but were now a dingy gray. Wide, brick steps climbed upward to a large, spacious porch. Two thick, heavy doors that resembled mahogany broke the lifeless monotony of the gray walls. '*Lifeless*,' the whole impressive structure emanated a forlorn, lonely look.

"Well, be yeh gittin'out, er aint ye?" The driver demanded. He leaned over and spat tobacco juice against the left front wheel, spattering the carriage steps.

"That'll be two dollars fer' tha ride, missy, an in good ol' U. S. uv' A. money, by golly! An none uv' thet wuthless paper, nuther! Ah h'aint gotna' use fer tha' stuff, nevah have, an nevah will! H'its gold or sili-ver fer ol' John Puckett evr' time, by golly!" He emphasized the words with another spatter of amber across the steps of the mansion. I sprang up from the carriage,

"Spit one more time across my steps, mister Puckett, and you will scrub every inch of them before I give you any of your money! And don't use anymore of your rude swear words in front of me again, do you hear me, Mr. Puckett! Mother and I, God rest her soul, lived in a house with four grown men. Neither she, nor I, ever tolerated such behavior in the presence of ladies'. And I do not intend to start now!"

The old saying goes, '*red hair, hot temper*.' I suppose in my case it was an understatement. Father had always said that he had been successful at most of the things in life, but curbing my temper was not one of them. The more he tried,

9

the worse it got, so he'd get around it by appealing to my seldom seen sense of humor. He would listen carefully to my fit of temper, all the while frowning darkly. Then, with his eyes belying everything with a twinkle, he would slam his fist down on his desk. Ink stand and quill-pen bouncing precipitously, he would stamp his huge booted foot. Then he would pretend to tear out his hair by the roots. No one ever born could have observed his antics and remained angry. My anger was always treacherously betrayed by a giggle. We always laughed uproariously, and then I would hug his neck and kiss the dear old thing.

'*Franklin had been right about it being an old eyesore,*' I thought. As Mr. Puckett off-loaded my baggage at the base of the plantation steps and with there being a lot of it, he grumbled under his breath something that sounded like,

"Dang Yankee females!" He glared thunderously. I ignored him.

'*Oh, it is an old monstrosity but I love it! It's beautiful!*' I was fascinated by the possibility of endless hours of exploration and discovery. I shivered deliciously. '*Perhaps I'd even meet a ghost! You're silly, Kelly Rhyman!*" I chided myself, '*Ghosts indeed!*' For the first time in weeks I had something to live for. This was to be mine if I decided to keep it. '*And Franklin's too!*' I reminded myself. I opened my parasol. The sun was quite hot.

A grunt, and a mumbled under-the-breath obscenity, I was sure, accompanied Mr. Puckett's announcement that this was the last of my bags.

"Could ah please beh' paid now an honest doller fer an honest job o' work? Ah' gotta be gittin' back ta town. Train'll be in agin' bout 6 oclock, more cus'mers." He puckered to spit, careful to do it in the driveway,

"Payin' un's!" He added impatiently.

10

"I know." I smiled, "It's my train." Puckett snorted,

"Huh, Shore!! "Well, I gotta git back or ol' Peabody'll be undercuttin me agin, the ol Bas...." Puckett fell silent as I impaled him with an icy stare. Sullenly, he watched as I dropped two silver dollars into the grimy, upturned palm. He grunted and climbed into the back into the carriage. I reached for my bags just as his spittle squirted loudly against the steps again. He whipped up the horses to spin out of the way of my parasol. Circling around and crunching gravel, he leaned out of the contraption to yell,

"Dang Yankee!" Then he disappeared down the lane in a cloud of dust. Guffaws like the braying of a donkey drifted back to my indignant ears. I shook my fist toward the dust and yelled angrily,

"If I ever see you again..." "Oh I'm so mad I could spit!" I walked across the driveway and picked up the parasol now red with Carolina dirt.

"Beggin' yoah pahdon, ma'am, but t'aint ladylike, spittin'!" A deep soft voice from somewhere behind me caused me to whirl around with wide eyes.

"Ooh! Where are you?" I asked, not really wanting to know.

"Right heah behine' thah doah, miss. Ah'll come out if'n its safe."

"Oh I guess it's safe." I assured the nameless voice behind the door, "unless your name is Puckett!" I added as a tall, strong-looking, Negro stepped from behind the door.

"Nope, ah'm Jeffuh'son." He smiled and made a great sweeping bow in my direction. "Pleased to make yo acquaintance, ma'am." He straightened and stepped carefully around the amber stains, then bowed again.

"Yo' be da new mistress, ah presume, ma'am? Ah' heard yo'all was ah comin'!"

11

"Yes, Mr. Jefferson? I am Miss Kelly Rhyman from Baltimore. I am here to assess the property and decide whether to sell or to renovate." Jefferson looked down at the ground, and then silently took two of my bags in his hand.

"Follah me, ma'am." We carefully ascended the steps. "Sho nuff, that ol' po' white trash Puckett done spit nuff' foah two, I reckon, sho' nuff!"

He set my bags down by the double doors then opened one of them to reveal a magnificent hallway. At the end of the hall I could see the lower portion of a great staircase.

"Ma'am, would yo' like to come into the ballroom and sit down?"

"Oh, yes, that would be best. I can wait there for the rest of my luggage if you don't mind.

"Laws' no, I was a gwanna git yo' baggage any ol' ways!" He turned to me and smiled a most sweet smile.

I was led through the high arched doors at the end of the hall. After seating me comfortably in a chair well-worn, Jefferson retired to bring in the rest of my bags.

I gazed with unbelief at richness that even I had never seen the equal of before. Rich yes, but now lusterless and neglected. The ceiling was high and reached far above the second floor where a Grand staircase wound downward to the floor of the ballroom.

'Talk about entrances,' I mused dreamily. A piano, grand of course, stood before a large, many framed, bay window. The window was at least fifteen or sixteen feet across and rose twelve or more above the black and white tile floor. A six foot French, crystal, chandelier hung downward over the ballroom. A ballustraded balcony led probably to back bedrooms. All the woodwork was oak or cypress and had wonderful carvings and elaborate designs that seemed to dance, leading your eyes around the room. Every wall had thickly carved bold moldings. An ornate and heavy candelabrum graced the piano's top side boards. I thought I could envision gold tin the woven drapery. The drapes needed cleaning, as did everything else I could see and observe. The urge to explore was more than I expected. Jefferson returned.

"Oh yes, Jefferson, you are the groom are you not?" I vaguely remembered father's attorney mentioning the presence of two former slaves who still lived here. They had remained loyal, staying behind after the others left.

"Yes'm, ah sho used to be. Now ah'm pahtly everthin'aroun' heah. Aint' no fine hosses left aft'uh ol' Dawkins got done sellin' em. Won' never know what com o' that money. Dawkins had a little, now and then, but didn't peer to be much." Jefferson cleared his throat.

"Welcome to Claibourne Manor, mistress, such as'tis. Ah been tryin' ta keep up da repairs, but s'awful hard, no money foah nails and all. Please be careful, ma'am." I smiled at him,

"Don't worry about me, Jefferson, I can take care of myself. And don't worry about Claibourne Manor; everything is going to be just fine!" Jefferson visibly brightened,

"Sho ma'am, aftuh seein' yo is quality folk, I done sho'nuff gwine takin' yo at yo word!" I followed him into the library. There, very comfortable looking chairs clustered before a great maw of a fireplace. Blackened bricks gave an indication of recent use.

"Do yo desire a bath, ma'am? Ah can have Callie fill da tub if, yo please. Baltimo sho'nuff fah frum heah, an' yo' must be tired." After my acceptance of his offer, he left to find Callie. I wandered slowly around the room. Over the mantle hung, a very, large portrait. A stern looking and dignified old gentleman stood clutching a large, wide brimmed hat. His hair and beard were white. A silk brocade vest complimented the black broadcloth suit. From a vest pocket dangled a gold watch chain. The eyes were black and seemed to penetrate the soul.

"Ah see yo all heve met tha Colonel, Miss Rhyman." Jefferson mumbled, "Ole Colonel J.C. Claibourne himself! Why, way that ol' gentleman carried on sometimes, folk used ta think thet he wuz half brother to tha devil his self!"

I followed Jefferson up the great winding staircase covered with a faded patterned carpet. He stalked down the upstairs hallway to a room that overlooked the garden. The room smelled musty and unused, but bright sunlight lit up the wallpapered walls. It streamed through double French doors which Jefferson opened wide.

"Need freash aih in heah, mistress. Ain't nobody used it since Miss June passed away, t'was her room. Colonel used ta come up here an' rock in dat ol' rockin' chair fo hours. Didn't pay ta bother him, them times. Thas' her theah, mum, she sho did love flowahs that women did. An' she was some great lady, too." Jefferson sighed.

The scent of Jasmine and magnolia blossoms filled the room from outside. The girl, Callie, was busy laying out my bath towels. She hardly glanced my way, as she was shy. After, I smiled in appreciation; I walked out onto the balcony.

"Oh Jefferson, is that honeysuckle?" I breathed.

"Yes'm tis! Mistress Claibourne loved it too. Ah always thought that she looked like a flower her own self ah' wearin' them bright an' pretty gowns o' hers. 'Course that wuz ah lot on account o' the Colonel. He always had ah way with tha ladies. But, Miss June, she done tamed him down. An' he loved evr' blessed minute of it! He used ta drink an' gamble, but he quit when miss June come 'long. She give him three fine strappin' sons befo' she died. Marse Lucas wuz the

14

oldest He wuz the old man's favorite. Old J.C. was lording' it around like he wuz God, his self, he wuz so happy. Course, all that wuz before the war, an' Seth an' Josh wuz killed by the Yankees, beggin' yo pardon ma'am. Jefferson went on,

"Ah remember when word came from town. Boy's names wuz posted 'long with others on th' wall o' th'courthouse. It seemed like Miss June up an' wilted like one o'her flowers she loved so well. Ol' Colonel wuz grievin', too but 'twernt nothin' compared to Miss June. She up an' died from the heartbreak! Ol' J.C. went plumb crazy then. He wouldn't let nobody touch her for two, maybe three days. I could hear him a'talkin'to her. An' I could heah him beggin' God to give her back to him, when God didn't, ol' J.C. shouted and raved, but death is death, an' he's jealous fer his price."

"Colonel Claibourne went back to his old ways, only wuss'! Drinkin' and walkin' round the house in the dead o' night. He killed a feller in a duel jest' cause the Colonel thought he insulted her memory! T'werent right, them doin's! The feller jus' said that Miss June had always been tha best lookin' gal in town. Colonel got mad 'cause he left out '*Lady*' and took it fer ah slight. One thin' fo sho', devil' all' us follows along hard times, but s'all in th' past now."

"Marse Lucas is th' only one left now, word was Lucas's troop o' Calvary got all wiped out! Ever' body cept Lucas! Deys wuz bodies ever' whar. When Lucas didn't turn up, folks said he was ah dayzuhter! Colonel went to town an' tried to find out who was malignin' his son. Nobody was dumb 'nuff to admit sayin' anythin'. But people still acted funny an ol' J.C. couldn't stand it no longer. Ah' found him out back, pistol in one hand. Miss June's picture in 'tother ah' layin' by her tomb, he wuz. Ol' Doc Morgan said maybe 'twas foah the bettah, Colonel wuz ah grievin' his self ta death. Anyways, he's with her now, Doc said, an' happy agin'. But they's some would say different!"

"Then Marse Lucas come home, mo' dead than alive." Jefferson recalled. "Me an' Callie done nuss'ed him back ta health. He said he 'scaped from one o' them prison camps. Nigh starved tuh' death, he wuz. Coase nobody believed him. Bunch o' fellah's jumped on him in town. His leg still weren't healed, and he didn't stand a chance. They beat him bad, an' it caused the leg ta' heal all wrong. Doc said t'werent nothing he could do."

"Then ol' Judge Hanson showed up wit'tha' sheriff, an' Sam Dawkins claimed that ol' J.C. done gwon an' cut Lucas out o'th will foah bein' a cowahd! Said he left ever'thin to Dawkins, th' po' white trash! Humph! Mark muh words, missy, ol' J.C. wouldn't a' left this place ta' th' likes o' him." Jefferson looked at me with dismay.

"Oh lawd, mistress, ah' done fo'got mah' mannahs, ah' beg yoah pahdon foah runnin'on so. Doan know what caused it less'n it's cause you reminded me o' Miss June. Sc'use me, ma'am, ah'll send Callie up wi'mo hot water."

Jefferson went out, calling for the girl Callie. I turned to the portrait on the wall. The former mistress of Claibourne Manor did bear a resemblance to me. The facial features were very similar, but where I had a certain healthy, tomboy look, this woman's features held a more wan, and delicate beauty. She was willowy, graceful. The blue eyes were haunting, but kind. The pale hands held a bouquet of violets and fern. She stood in a pale blue gown with a gossamer quality. Her honey-golden hair looked to be stirred by the wind, perhaps.

I could see why the colonel had been obsessed by this woman. She was radiant, but at the same time she had a little girl quality that would make a man want to die protecting her. Yes, there was some resemblance, but my hair was red. Her body had a frail, feminine aura. Nobody ever said mine was anything but strong and healthy. There was nothing in me that could touch this woman's strange, alluring beauty.

I turned to the view of the garden. I leaned on the banister and gazed at the colorful, blossoming plants. The air was heady, intoxicating! I was already hypnotized, fascinated. Father would have chided me with being an emotional female. *'No place for sentiments in business!'*

Callie and Jefferson arrived with the water. Warm steam filled the room.

"We'uns will take oah leave now missy, if'n yo please, ma'am."

"Just one more thing, Jefferson, I'm curious about this, "Lucas", you mentioned. Is he going to contest the will do you suppose? I understand that he was the eldest son. How could anyone just give up his home without a fight?"
'Perhaps this "Lucas" character was a coward', I speculated to myself. Jefferson cleared his throat.

"Well, Miss Rhyman, you nevah met Mars Lucas oah you wouldn't have ta ask them questions. When the judge and Sam tol' Marse Lucas he'd better leave or go to jail, Marse left foah show. But he looked all three o'them in the eye, an' tol' em to thank God foah the war. Said he could kill 'em all but he'd seen 'nuff killin! I thinks maybe Marse Lucas, *'wuz a grievin',* just like his ol' man. Sometimes when he come 'roun', I'd let him in real quiet like so's he could visit his folks down yondah in th' graveyard. Ol' Dawkins woulda' had a fit if'n he'd knowd ah done it!" Jefferson grinned.

"Will that be all, Miss Rhyman?"

"Yes, Jefferson, and tell Callie I said thank you."

"Oh, yes, mum, thank you, ma'am."

Jefferson went out with his long, loose limbed stride. I waited a moment until his footsteps faded down the hall.

17

Then I went over and locked the door. After all, I was a lone woman in a strange place. The trip had been long, dusty and hot. All I wanted now was my bath, and then a nap before dinner. Stupid me! I hadn't asked what time dinner would be.

'*Oh well, Kelly, Ol' girl, Jefferson or Callie will just have to knock, I guess.*' I undressed quickly after closing the French doors and drapes. It was a temptation to leave them open, and let the warm breeze blow softly into the room. '*Not today!*' I promised myself, '*But maybe another time!*'

Later, after a good long soak, I got into bed and felt the day's tension leave my body. I thought about Jefferson. It seemed as if he'd been relieving his soul of all that troubles him. The story he'd related to me was tragic but only one of many caused by the war. Then the feather mattress and the warm coverlet sent my senses into oblivion.

3
~Sam Dawkins~

I was awakened a short while later to shouting somewhere down below. I could hear Jefferson's deep bass voice arguing insistently with someone. Hurriedly, throwing on a bathrobe and slippers, I padded silently down the hall. The voices because more audible.

"Ah must insist, Suh! The mistress is asleep an' haint to be distuhbed by the likes o' yo! Po' white trash! Now, go on an' git a'fore ah throws yo' out!" I hurried to descend the staircase while a voice, course with anger, rang out.

"Yall just try it, Niggah! Ah'll whup yo within an inch o' yore mizable black life! Uppity! Ah'm heah to see th' female on bizness an' taint none o' your'n. Ah used to show you all who's boss and I kin agin, yessuh! Stan' back, ah say!"

The speaker was a large, bearded man who looked to be in his forties. Unkempt brown hair thrust out from beneath a sweat-grimed hat. His jaw was thrust out, the beard quivering with rage. Spittle sprayed as the wild-eyed brute raised a black snake whip to strike Jefferson.

"Git out o'mah way, niggah! He angrily shouted at Jefferson, "Git out o' mah way, now!"

I seen that he was about to strike Jefferson, so acting fast I called out loudly,

"Enough of this! That will be quite enough! Explain yourself, sir, for this rude and boorish intrusion!"

"Dawkins, ma'am, ah'm Sam Dawkins." The man looked at Jefferson gloatingly, and then turned to me suggestively.

"Ah'm heah to talk to you on bizness, ma'am, an 'in private, if'n you don't mind!" He glared back at Jefferson with insolence.

"Oh but, I do mind, Mr. Dawkins. Whatever you wish to say to me you may say in front of my groom, Mr. Jefferson. He is in my employ and I expect him to remain as before, a very trusted member of this household!" Jefferson visibly grew taller. I could see a very determined glint in his eyes. He gazed unblinkingly at Dawkins. Sam Dawkins puffed with indignation.

"Ah'll have you know thet ah been over-seer o' this heah plantation fer nigh onto fifteen yeahs. Th' ol man done up an' shot himself, an left 'er to me, lock, stock, an barrel!" Course that wuz before yore pappy done cheated me out of it, yessuh! Ah' ain't neveh seen nobody roun' these parts that 'llows theah niggas to know theah bizness! Yo got ah lot ta learn missy, a'fore you kin come down heah an' boss us good southerners around! Yankees all' us tryin' to tell us what to do, yassuh!"

"Mr. Dawkins! I'll mind you to hold your filthy tongue! I assure you that whatever business you wanted to discuss with me I most certainly am not interested in! I give you fair warning, sir! If you ever show your face around here again, or lift a hand toward anyone in my employ, you will live to regret it! Mark well what I say, if I ever hear of you maligning the good name of my father, I sir, shall show you how a Yankee can shoot! I shall put an end to your miserable life, now get out!"Jefferson stepped toward Dawkins,

"Yo heard tha mistress, Suh! Get on out o'heah or Ah'll..." the click of the small pistol cocking was loud enough to gain attention from them both! I said no more,

20

anger made me tremble slightly. Dawkins blanched. The small round eye of the gun held straight and true.

"N-now ma'am, take it easy with that, now, ah apologize, ah'm ah'goin..." Then he turned and bolted out the door. The man's whining deprecatory voice lingered in my consciousness even after the rapid hoof beats of his departure faded into the distance.

"Despicable! Such a cur!" Suddenly, I came to myself. Jefferson's eyes were wide with a strange look. He smiled,

"An' good riddance ta po' white trash!" His booming laughter echoed through the old mansion. I uncocked the revolver and placed it back into the pocket of my robe.

"I shall go and make myself presentable, Jefferson, and then I shall go to the garden. Will you please call me when dinner is served?" Jefferson glowed,

"Sho' miss, an' may ah offah mah congratulations, please ma'am?"

"What in heaven's for, Jefferson?"

"Well now, missy," he began, "ah said sho nuff you all remind me of Mistress June. But, in some ways, you haint like huh a-tall, naw Suh! Jefferson retreated down the hall. I heard him call to Callie somewhere in the recesses of the mansion,

"Callie gurl, come heah! We uns got us a sho'nuff lady fer a mistress! But she sho' is ah fire-eaten one!

'Oh well, times a' wasting, Kelly ol' girl, let's go!' The phrase oft' spoken by my father brought a pang to my heart. When I got to my room, I sat down and felt the hot tears flow quietly down my cheeks.

'Daddy, I miss you so! I lost my temper again, but I did not like that man!' Somehow I felt that this time father would have agreed with me. I never saw him back down from any man. He was proud and stern with those who worked for him.

Railroad men were generally strong men. My father worked his way up the ladder, and became one of the most respected in the industry. His passing had left Franklin and me very wealthy. However, I would forfeit all of it if I could hear dad's booming laughter and have him back again.

'*Franklin will be coming soon,*' I thought, '*but he won't stay long. He can't stay away from Baltimore for very long. I have a feeling that I'm about to lose my dear brother to matrimony. That could be fun!*'

I dressed quickly, and then softly and slowly descended the stairs. I still had the delicious thrill of exploring the mansion before me. But that could wait. I wanted to be outside at this time of the evening. The garden pulled me like a magnet. I walked along the path, touching and smelling the blossoms. All manner of flowers were present. Roses, Chrysanthemums, Baby's Breath, Irises, and many more that I did not remember seeing before. There was a section where only herbs were growing. There was the familiar smell of mint. This had been used to make the wonderful julep tea that I had tasted before on a business trip with my father. I thought the cool, refreshing beverage delightful, '*I'll ask Callie to please make me some.*'

Feeling much better out in the coolness, I looked all around me. '*Oh, what a grand, romantic place this plantation must have been before the war!*' A gray stone statue of a child and a fawn stood in the center of the garden. Looking closer, I could see an opening in the vessel of the statue. I realized that this must have been the mouth of the beautiful fountain. Water stains were faded and camouflaged by moss and algae. A large stone basin encircled the statue. I continued on my way very slowly, drinking in the atmosphere of a world known to a select generation of people. But now, it was all gone forever. The atmosphere I breathed was ancient, and yet brand-new. I looked wondrously and pictured how this old plantation must have shown for three generations.

'*Chivalry had lived here, and shame,*' I thought, thinking of the Negroes, singing the ballads and hymns so rending to the heart. I could see the proud, militant old Colonel as he stalked about among his guests on the veranda. He greeted each in turn, speaking to the gentlemen and bowing to the ladies. I could almost hear the rustling of silk and crinoline. There would be music, wonderful music that signaled the gentlemen to choose their partners for the next waltz. Toasts were held aloft in white gloved hands.

"God save the south, and preserve her dignity!" the old Colonel's voice range out thunderously. I could hear the bubbling, fluid music of the fountain's stream gushing from the vessel held in the arms of the child. The fawn stretched forth its neck to drink from the stream. While overhead the great fountain shot into the air, sparkling in the evening light. Lily pads floated in the stone pool. The yellow, dewy blossoms reflected on the dark waters. Goldfish darted about, along with the occasional frog. I heard the katydids, or thought I did, for now it was getting quite late in the evening. The sun was about down.

Jefferson had not yet called. I found myself quite suddenly and a little nervously, in front of the well-kept cemetery. Lilac bushes bordered its edge, and a slightly rusty iron gate barred the way. I leaned a hand on its top and leaned forward. Fresh flowers on the graves bore testimony of love and care. I thought of the oldest son, Lucas.

'*What manner of man was he? What would he think of me? Oh well, I'd cross that bridge when I came to it.*'

I opened the gate to stand before the great stone crypt. The plaque read:

"Col. Jasper Calhoun Claibourne"
1812-1864

Just below it were the words:

"Alicia June Claibourne"
1819-1863
"Beloved mistress of Claibourne Manor.
Heavenly Angels greet her as a loving wife and mother.
Amen."

I glanced at the neat row of white marble tombstones. Each held an epitaph.

"Why do people put verses on tomb stones?" I said aloud, for no reason.

"Perhaps, to ease their guilty conscience," A voice answered!

'Ooh!' I felt fear clutch my throat! I felt like turning to run from the unseen presence! The voice had seemed to emanate from the very ground! My heart threatened to pound the breath from my lungs! With wide eyes, I observed as a dirt encrusted hand emerged from around the largest of the gravestones! It slowly gripped the top, as if the dead corpse was dragging itself from its moldy prison! I quite regretfully remembered my small pistol. It now nestled upstairs in the pocket of my robe! Terror mounted in my breast! Green grass stains mingled amongst the dirt granules on the creeping grasping hand. I decided that I would not scream. I opened my mouth!

"JEFF-ERSON!" Well! It still sounded like a scream. I stood rooted to the spot. The groping hand became an arm, and then the apparition stood on its feet!

24

4

~Marse Lucas Claibourne~

The '*apparition*' quite obviously, was male, approximately six feet or so. He was muscular and over tanned. For a '*corpse*' he was quite handsome. There was a well-trimmed mustache and beard. The hair was a light golden brown but the beard was dark with a tinge of red. White teeth flashed in a smile that was half humorous, and half sarcastic. The black, well-set eyes topped a countenance vaguely familiar to me.

"Well now, foah one of the conquering Yankee cah-pet baggah's, ah must admit that you'ah not exactly what ah had in mind! Ah imagined yo'ah to be much mo'ah impo'sin foah one of the occupin' fo'ces!"

'*Oh!*' Not only had this insolent rogue frightened me half out of my wits, but now he was insulting me, also!

"You sir, are a trespasser, and an insulting one at that! I demand to know what you are doing here in my cemetery and on my property." '*There! That should put the scoundrel in his place! Any moment now, he should apologize!*'

"Oh, ah do beg yoah pahdon, ma'am, ah was not away-yah of any rich Yankees bein' buried heah! Could you-all please direct me to whe-ah they lay, ma'am?

"Ohh, you manner less ruffian, I remind you that I can have you arrested, sir! You are both insulting and coarse!"

25

The strangers smile still flashed with obvious sarcastic humor. In a moment, I should lose control!

"We shall see, sir, if you smile, when my groom Jefferson arrives! He is quite strong, and I shall have him throw you bodily from my property!"

The disturbing black eyes focused on something in the back of me. Then, his vibrant voice announced.

"Of coahse, ma'am, ahh do believe this is the gentleman comin' now." I turned to see Jefferson striding up purposefully.

"You-all called foah me, Miss Rhyman?"

"Yes, Jefferson, I have apprehended this-this, uncivilized interloper trespassing upon my property! I wish you to beat him to within an inch of his cowardly life, and then throw him from the premises!" Quite suddenly, the stranger's smile was gone. It was replaced by a glittering flash of lightning from those black eyes. Whether it was something I had said, or the threat of bodily harm, I could not say. I had to tear my gaze away from those terrible black eyes!

"Well Jefferson?" I demanded. Jefferson blanched. His mouth dropped open, appalled. The trespasser smiled at him, and then he turned to again to look at me, the smile disappearing like a thistle in the wind.

"Ah nevah once claimed to be ah man with no faults, but bein' ah cow-ahd is not one of them! If yoah were ah man, ah would exact payment foah that accusation, ma'am!"

"Oh you would, would you? Then pray tell me, sir, what kind of man goes around frightening poor innocent females and hiding behind tombstones?" I asked all the while fighting back my temper.

"Oh, did ah scayeh, you all ma'am? Ah'm so sorry, ah' beg youah eveh-lastin' foah-giveness, then."

26

"I was only startled for a moment, sir! It would take quite a lot more than the likes of you to, frighten me!"

"Well, ma'am, it did seem to me that yo-all called foah yoah man Jefferson quite loudly! Of coase, ah will admit that yo-all didn't scream, o-ah swoon like most o' these infuhnal females thet ah have obsuved aroun' heah. Ah nevah could stand th' screamin', helpless, clingin' vine type!"

"Jefferson!"

"Yes ma'am?" What are you waiting for?"

"O' lawd Miss Rhyman, yo doan undah'stan, ahh can't!"

"What, Jefferson? Do you mean to imply that you would stand there and let me be insulted and taken advantage of by a, a, criminal, like this?"

"No Ma'am, ah wouldn't let nobody mistreat you missy, an' no 'bout that paht 'bout him bein' a criminal! Ma'am, he ain' no criminal, foah sho! This heah is mah fo-mah mastuh Marse Lucas Claibourne, an' he has always been mah friend!"

I wanted to sink into the ground. My temper had gotten me into trouble again. This man Lucas was the person who really had a right to be present on this hallowed ground. I had called him a criminal! But he called me a carpetbagger! My sense of justice reasoned. He was simply infuriating! Confident! My conscience shot back, and remember this was his home! Oh, what to do?

"Beggin yoah pahdon, ma'am, but dinnah is served, such as 'tis." Jefferson rescued me! "Thesah's been no cook 'roun heah since the Dawkins left. Me an' Callie been makin' do. Doan know if'n yo gwan to live an' stand it, foah sho." Jefferson fidgeted. He obviously wanted me to invite Lucas to dinner, but I was still at a loss even to look at the man. I stuttered.

"W-well I" Mr. Claibourne rescued me this time.

"Oh, do excuse me, miss-tress Rhyman, ah must take mah leave of yo-all now! Ah have a mos' pressin' engagement. Ah do hope yo-all will foa-give me foah mah bad mannuhs an' trespassin! Ah bid yo good evenin', Miss Rhyman." He nodded to Jefferson.

My antagonist gallantly stepped forward to bow and kiss my hand. Marse Lucas Claibourne strode purposefully away, limping slightly. I had not noticed the cane until now.

Jefferson called me three times before I answered.

"Ma'am, please ma'am? Ayah yo-all comin', Miss Rhyman?" Red faced and flustered, I replied,

"Oh yes, thank you Jefferson."

"Doan thank me ma'am, th' co'n pone is burnt, an' th' vegetables half done. Lordy, that Callie-girl jest haint no cook foah sho!"

Any regrets that I had not invited Lucas to dinner dissipated as soon as I tasted dinner. Jefferson's evaluation of Callie's culinary talents was more kind than truthful. Most of the meal was left. Feingin not to be too hungry, I spared her feelings if possible. Obviously, if I kept this place, I should have to hire a cook. I abhorred cooking. Mother died before I was old enough to get serious about it. My talents in the kitchen also were neglected due to a doting spoiling father. I should have to inquire about available help in town. Surely good wages would solve the problem.

I had made my decision! No matter what Franklin should say. Guiltily, I believed that I knew what his reaction would be. No matter, I now knew that it would break my heart to part with the old plantation. I needed it! I felt at home here, more than Baltimore with all the lawyers and business people. Of course, I wasn't able to turn loose of everything. I should simply travel back and forth, and use the telegraph! I shall restore to this grand old house her former glory!

Fortunately, my almost unlimited funds should more than accomplish the task. It should prove to be a most agreeable and challenging endeavor.

I'll need new drapes, lumber and whitewash. I must hire workers and laborers. Skilled artisans were harder to find. The garden must be pruned, and the fountain connected again! The stables, *'oh, how much fun I was going to have fixing those complete with new straw, after a good thorough cleaning, of course! I should send for some of my beloved horses from Baltimore.'*

I sat well into the night, preparing lists and plans. Tomorrow, I intended to see everything, know everything, about Claibourne Manor Plantation! There was so much to be done. Perversely, I wondered what Lucas Claibourne would think about all this. Would he be pleased?

'How should I care?' I sniffed. *'The man was obviously jealous and resentful of me. Carpetbagger! But why should I care what a coward thinks, or says?'* I fumed, *'Could I help it if his father had disinherited him? Did I start the war? No! South Carolina had begun the bloody, horrible conflict. In a way,'* I reasoned unfairly, *'Lucas Claibourne was partly to blame!'*

I rushed to leap into the feather mattress, snuggling down into the warm coverlet. It was quite a while before I slept. I kept seeing dark, fathomless eyes first blazing with anger, then deeply sad and accusing! I suddenly realized the reason for Lucas's dirty hands. He was the one who kept the garden and cemetery. He had been planting flowers, probably on one of his brother's graves. Perhaps I should visit him, wherever he was now staying. I should take Jefferson, of course, to keep tongues from wagging. I wasn't about to start off in my new home by obtaining a doubtful reputation. Besides, it was just to apologize for my misunderstanding.

29

'Oh drat! Must I stay awake all night thinking about the man! He was nothing to me!'

5

~Teresa~

Tomorrow! It took me almost a week to tour, examine, tally, and make endless notes of repair and acquisitional needs for the old monstrosity. There was over five thousand acres of land, streams, and a pond. A couple of thousand more in forest land. There were old run-down slave cabins. There was a grist mill, a cane press, an orchard and a cider mill. The dam for the grist mill had to be repaired and the spill-o-way reconnected. A saw mill and a brick kiln showing long disuse. The blade was rusty, as was the rest of the machinery. Horse and mule power had been the prevalent energy, except for the obvious slave labor. There were no crops, only weedy, overgrown fields with occasional naturally seeded odd plants growing here and there. I am afraid that fathers little rich girl soon became quite bedraggled and soiled.

I had Jackson remove all the utensils and household items for repair to a shed next to the blacksmith shop. Broken tools created a pile awaiting the forges hot glow. Callie's services as a washerwoman were stretched to the limit. She, Jefferson, and I dusted and polished until the old house began to be live able again. For some reason, I could not bear to part with any but the absolutely hopeless items.

'I want to keep everything as close as possible to the original decor, for Lucas' sake.' I absently reasoned. *'I don't want to appear to be destroying his home. Ridiculous, Lucas*

31

does not live here anymore!' I fumed!

But I was wrong! Later, while riding on one of the farthest reaches of the forest land, I spied smoke coming from one of the former woodcutter's cabins chimney. There was a horse standing outside the wooden steps. It was quite a nice horse, clad with a sidesaddle. This was obviously a woman's horse.

'Now what would a woman's horse be doing with a fire in my woodcarver's cabin?' I was determined to find out. I rode right up to the door, and challenged whoever was in the house.

"Whoever is in there, you had better come out for this is my land, and you are trespassing!" I held my horse's reins in my left hand, while my right clutched the small pistol in my pocket. The door to the cabin opened with a groan and out stepped Lucas Claibourne!

"Ohh, Mr. Claibourne! I did not expect it to be you sir! I observed the horse and sidesaddle, and was expecting a woman!"

"Good evening Miss-tress Rhyman," Lucas' smile still had that peculiar humorous yet sarcastic quality. "Wont yo-all come in? Since this heah is, aftah all, yo-ah property, ma'am." Those eyes looked into my soul.

I was suddenly aware of my dirty and bedraggled appearance. Which I imagined must present a very different picture from the woman he was used to seeing.

"My apologies sir for my appearance, I didn't expect to meet you again so soon. Jefferson gave me no warning, you see. However, I do wish to apologize to you for the outrageous treatment I subjected you to."

But before Lucas could answer, a lady in voluminous dress and pantaloons stepped from the doorway to stand beside him. She was quite lovely, with deep brown eyes and cameo skin. Her dark hair was topped by a fine ribboned riding hat. She was pinning the hat to her auburn curls,

"And what treatment was that?" the lady replied, giving me a disdainful look and a sniff.

"May ah introduce y'all two ladies seein' as how yo-all are nei-bahs and all?" Lucas stated matter-of-factly. "Teresa this heah is the new mistress of Claibourne Manor Plantation, Miss Kelly Rhyman. Miss Rhyman, Teresa Baynes, yoah neih'bah! Miss Baynes was kind enough to bring me a nice picnic lunch. It so was quite tasty, Miss Baynes. Ah'm foh-evah in yoah debt!"

The look the woman gave Lucas was the most cat-in-the-catnip-patch gaze I had ever witnessed. She checked again to make sure that she was again presentable. I was sure that a minute ago she had not been! After she had made sure of the fact that I had noticed, she unsheathed her claws.

"Mistuh Claibourne, do be tha puhfect gentlemen that you ahh, an' help me to mount mah hoase, if you please." She smiled sweetly at me and added, "Miss Kelly is that yoah name? It sounds quite manly don't you think? You really must come ovah and visit sometime. But please do not ride astride. Heah in tha south, all us la-dies ride sidesaddle!

There it was! She flung the insult as a direct challenge.

"Oh really, Miss Baynes, and do Ladies here in the south, also come to gentlemen's cabins unchaperoned?" I replied quite innocently.

"I really must find out all I can about your southern manners, you know!"

"Of coahse especially the need foah takin' baths!" She countered with a sniff.

"Oh dear I do believe I see a snake!" I stared intently into the grass beside her horses hooves.

"Oooh!" Teresa gasped, looking down fearfully, "Wheah,

33

foah goodness sakes?"

"There!" I jerked my pistol from my pocket and fired instantly into the grass. POW! Her cat's claws were not sufficient for her to retain her precarious seat on her, whinnying, rearing mount. Teresa turned a beautiful backward somersault, flying pantaloons must have been a great help upon her contact with the ground. She sat dazedly until Lucas rushed to her side.

"Teresa! Aah yo' all right? Ah do hope thet yo'ah not injured, ma'am." He helped her gingerly to her feet. Teresa brushed at the dirt on her dress.

"Ouch," she whined piteously, rubbing her backside. "You did that on puhpose, you- you-..."

"Of course, I always shoot snakes on purpose," I said, searching the grass with my eyes. "But I must have missed this one. It was the side saddle." I added. "They are quite unsafe, especially here in the woods where snakes live." I turned my own mount toward home. "You really must hurry home for a bath, Teresa. You look a might disheveled, you know. Bye!" I said sweetly, avoiding Lucas' icy stare.

6
~Post War Columbia~

"**G**ood mownin' Miss Rhyman, yo-all sho is up early. This heah is sho goin' to be ah fine day, a fine day!"

"Good morning, Jefferson, I certainly hope so. I am packed and ready to go. How far is it to Columbia?"

"Mos' fawty mile o' so, missy, I done greased up the axles of the buggy." I studied the paint chipped dilapidated contraption. Jefferson started taking harness down from the wall.

"Now, doan yo worry, Miss Rhyman, I's takin tools an' ah spare wheel. Dis ol' buggy, she aint bright an' fancy no mo, but she'll git us theah right nuff!"

"Excellent, Jefferson, but you may call me Kelly."

"Oh no, mistress, dat wouldn't be fitten' foah me to call yo by yo fust name, no, ma'am." Jefferson led one of the few horses still left into the buggy shafts. The animal was a sorrel gelding about 15 hands from his large hooves to this withers. The horse fidgeted and rolled his eyes.

"Coo now, ol hoss." Jefferson soothed in a low, whisper soft voice. "Coo now! S'been ahh long time foah him missy, but he's the bes'o'dems dats left!" I could tell that Jefferson had a way with horses. Just wait till he saw those in Baltimore! Today I shall send for some of them! The telegraph office was only one of the many places I planned to visit today!

The buggy wheels crunched on the gravel drive. We were

on our way! Of course it should take longer than if the carriage were drawn by John Puckett's pair of matched bays. I comment on this to Jefferson.

"Yes ma'am, them bays is fine hoss flesh. They is part o' th' blooded stock tha' Colonel raised. He sho' did love dem hosses. He tu'n ovah in he grave if'n he knowed John Puckett gots em'! The bes' stock wuz sold off by no count' Dawkins foah money to buy whiskey. He waz bad 'nuff when he wuz de overseer foah de colonel. Latuh on, when he's posed to own de place, he got even mo downright mean. De only thing what kep' me goin' wuz I's borned an' raised on dis land. An' ah is g'wine to see'er through to de end. Couhse, ah done had de dream!" Jefferson beamed.

"What dream, Jefferson?"

"Oh I's done seen de ol' place, de plantation, in de dream, she shine lihke old times, eben finah, an' Marse Lucas, he wuz happy agin!"

Columbia was not the town that it had been before the war. A few blackened, burned buildings bore mute testimony of the ravaging of the union army. Most of the people wore hallowed masks of hopelessness. Poverty, tragedy, pain, and despair still burned the southerner's hearts with a flame inextinguishable. I tried not to stare at the most obviously unfortunate. Oh how it tore my heart to see the children, the poor little children. Although the war was two years gone, the suffering went on for a people that still fought for life and dignity. Their army was defeated, but the people still stood proud and defiant. They stood no more in silks or tailored suits. No more did livery coachmen await their mistresses before imported finery shops. No more were the streets lined with carriages of shining brass and velvet seats. Although worn and patched apparel was now the rule, the spirit of defiance burned in the eyes level and straight.

This was no humbled, down trodden folk with lowered countenance. "Uncle" Robert had signed papers of surrender, but in each southern heart, burned the declaration of defiance! *'Not me, not me!'*

Some would move westward, others would stay and try to rebuild shattered dreams. But one dream was dead. It lay in ashes, shattered beyond repair. The shards scattered and lost in hardened, red clods of uncultivated fields. It lay beside its King, *'King Cotton'*, which no more filled warehouses, railway cars, riverboats and ocean vessels. The idealistic, chivalrous dream of the old south lay dead at the feet of a greater, prouder, dream, the dream, of an undivided nation with a stronger, more definite idealism, the idealism of equality and non-slavery.

Heaven cannot be heaven for only a few. It must be heaven for all, or else it is not heaven. I held one of the shards of the dream, the whole should never be again, but I should polish the shard as a memorial to a fallen hero, the hero of a brave, shining, southern way of life. It would not be easy. I would be seen as an enemy. Hatred and resentment were foes to be defeated. I must win the peoples trust. I must win their acceptance. I shall begin with Lucas Claibourne!

Jefferson unloaded my bags in front of the hotel. Upon my suggestion that he take a room, also, he grinned at my naiveté,

"No'm, not just yet, mebbe' someday. Mr. Lincoln set us free, but we'uns haint dat free. Dis heah is still de south. An'us black folk still got our place. Ah'm goin down to de stable an'bed down in de straw. Ah's gonna find us some fine hoss flesh an' de fanciest surry dey gots in dis town. Ah'll fetch yo' in de 'mawnin, bright an' early, Miss Rhyman. Yo takes care, now. Like ah say, dis heah is still de south!"

Jefferson did not add the obvious, *'an'yo is still ah'*

Yankee!' Somehow, it was apparent. The innkeeper, after reassuring himself that the *'Niggah'* was not going to ask for a room, allowed me to sign the register and obtain the key. Cash in advance was the rule for all. I must arrange my financial affairs tomorrow, as well as register the deed in mine and Franklin's names at the land office. I should also wire my attorney. Father had several in his law firm. The desire was to aquire the services of someone in Columbia known to them.

While planning to demand immediate answer via the telegraph, I ate the bread and canned vegetable from my basket, and then I had a quick sponge bath with the water in the chipped pitcher on the wash stand. The bowl and basin' did not match. Both were of a different pattern and color.

While retiring for the night in the iron bedstead, of course my little pistol went under my pillow. Sleep came fitfully. The noise of wagons and voices did not cease until far into the night. The bank was not to open until ten a.m. the next day. The telegraph office opened at eight.

Early at 8 am, I sent a message to our law firm directing them of the amount of money that I wanted transferred to the local bank. While I waited for the return message Jefferson and I would partake of breakfast in the culinary establishment across the street. Entering confidently but definitely alone, all my efforts to get Jefferson to accompany me had been to no avail. A, *'No Nigra's Served,'* sign hung over the door declared the terrible prejudice still holding firm. My message awaited me one hour later. I was to contact a man by the name of Alexander Robbins of Robbins and Son Law offices.

Alex Robbins was a tall, sandy haired young man just five years out of law school. I liked him immediately. The elder Robbins was away on business in Charleston. The younger Alex read my letter of introduction swiftly.

"Miss Kelly Rhyman, of Rhyman and sons," He arched his brow, "a very reputable company, and there are other interests and chattels are there not? I have heard dad speak of your father, Miss Rhyman, and the sons? They are your brothers of course. Oh, I'm so sorry, I must apologize. Forgive me but I need to be clear on everything. You have only one brother surviving now. You and Franklin I believe, inherit the estate?"

"Yes, Mr. Robbins, you are correct." I then explained to him my situation and the plans for Claibourne Manor Plantation. "Your Firm is highly recommended by my attorneys in Baltimore. I desire someone quite more *'at hand,'* if you please, than Baltimore. I also desire to complete my affairs here in Columbia, today if possible." Alex Robbins beamed,

"The lady's wish is my command! I have a few small matters to clear with my secretary, and I shall be free and at your disposal, Miss Rhyman." He stepped outside, leaving the door ajar. *'I think he will do. Oh, yes, I think Mr. Robbins will do nicely.'*

It took only a short while to arrange for the transfer of the deed. Franklin and I were now the legal owners of Claibourne Manor Plantation. Only one more task remained to complete, and then I should be able to begin my own reconstruction. The teller behind the window at the bank ushered Mr. Robbins and I into the President's office. His honor, Judge Lowell P. Hansen quickly bade us to be seated. He was a balding, portly gentleman who smoked a cigar vigorously and wore gold-rimmed spectacles. When informed of my business and identity, he patted my hand ingratiatingly. He was all smiles when he learned of the amount to be transferred to his bank. Alex Robbins explained the particulars for my servant's wages, and that I wished for my hand written drafts to be paid in demand upon presentation.

"And who, may I ask, are these people?" The judge poised pen over paper. I told him,

"Jefferson and a young girl by the name of Callie." He wrote swiftly.

"And where have you decided to take up residence, if you please, Miss Rhyman? I can be of great assistance, if you perchance are looking to buy. I have many valuable assets in real estate, and I..." Interrupting, I stated,

"I have already acquired a small, shall we say, estate?" The judge was visibly disappointed.

"Oh, so you have, and where is it located?" He gazed at me over his spectacles like a wise old owl. The cigar stuck out sideways between clenched teeth.

"Claibourne Manor Plantation," He sputtered, allowing the cigar to drop to the top of the desk. Sparks flew at random. Alex and I both rose dexterously, pushing back our chairs. I brushed at my dress and shawl.

"Excuse me, excuse me, I, er, I.... But it is quite impossible. Claibourne Manor Plantation belongs to a gentleman by the name of Samuel Dawkins. It is quite my understanding that it is not for sale, at any price!" The judge stood up.

"You are correct. It was not for sale. Nor did I buy it."

"Then how did you aquire the property?" The judge's face was red, whether from the cigar or something else, I could not tell.

"Samuel Dawkins was an orphan. He had no next of kin, or so I have heard." The judge looked as if he was apoplectic.

"Very true, sir, I inherited the deed from my father. I am sure that you have heard the name John Jacob Rhyman?"

"Hah yes, but how did he obtain the deed?" his honor threw away the cigar with an exasperated gesture.

"He won it in a poker game, sir. I believe, from this same Samuel Dawkins you speak of."

"Aah..., gambling!" His honor peered at me over the top of the gold-rimmed spectacles. "I believe that wagering is illegal in this county. That would make the transaction worthless, would it not?" His honor drew himself up and tucked his thumbs behind his silk brocade vest.

Alex Robbins smiled wolfishly.

"Of course, if the game had taken place in this county. However, the transaction or wager transpired in the City of Charleston. I believe that in Charleston, as you know sir, it's quite legal and collectable by law. In return, of course, if a likewise valuable wager is offered in exchange."

"But the property is in this county!" The judge protested.

"It makes no difference, sir!" Alex shot back. "Only the place of wager is relevant, not the location of the property. State law up holds the legality of gambling debts as long as they take place in a municipality of legalized gambling, and even across state lines where necessary! Any chattel or property may be seized as long as it is wagered in a legal precinct of the state, or states, if you wish." Alex Robbins placed his briefcase on the judges desktop and unsnapped the lid.

"I have the volume containing the item in question right here, sir, if you please. And well marked, sir, well marked!"

His honor waved a placating, pudgy hand. I noticed the yellow stain of tobacco and nicotine around the nails. "No, sir, not necessary, not necessary at all, I do believe that I do recall the, er, statute you speak of, sir, yes sir, I certainly do! Ah yes, Miss Rhyman, is there anything else that I can do for you today?"

"I shall require a legal agreement of the deposit, and guaranteed tendering, sir, on default of the bank if any discrepancy is found as to the amount or the person involved. "I am sure that you agree with me that an institution should uphold its integrity by standing behind its employees?" His honor had bridled at the veiled implication of incompetency, or perhaps, something worse. He said,

"Of course."

Alex winked at me and produced the document. The judge was again his ingratiating self.

"Thank you, again Miss Rhyman, Please feel free to call on me anytime, anytime at all. I personally guarantee you that you shall receive extraordinary service, extra ordinary!" He repeated assuredly.

As we crossed the street to Alex's office, I looked at him quizzically,

"How did you know that I would ask for a document of assurance?" he again gave that knowing, wolfishly grin.

"I am afraid that you are not exactly a stranger to me, Miss Rhyman. I have heard so much about you from my father," he explained, "from our business dealings. And I must confess that you are a chip off the old block!"

"Well," I sniffed, "Father!" Alex gave that toothy grin again.

"Oh yes, before I forget. I sat in on that poker game with your father."

"Yes?" I absently queried, thinking that Alex Robbins was quite good-looking when he smiled like that.

"I am afraid that the wager your father made against the plantation was not of equal value!" I laughed.

"He would not have considered it good business, sir, if it had been!" Alex took my hand in his.

"I shall be calling upon you at times, Miss Rhyman, on

business of course." He added with a twinkle.

"Of course!" I agreed turning to go. I looked back over my shoulder at the young attorney, "On business," as I stepped into the street.

"Lookout Miss Rhyman!" I turned to see a heavy freight wagon bearing down on me. Foam flew from the horse's open mouths. Yellow teeth were plainly visible. The juggernaut's wheels threw geysers of red dust into the air behind it. I opened my mouth to scream and was struck. The crushing, grinding sound of the wheels whirred past my head as pain and lights flashed in my brain. I heard someone yell for help.

"Somebody get ol' doc' Morgan, quick!" Then sweet merciful darkness plunged me into oblivion.

7

~The Business Woman~

'*Oooh...* ' I could smell various odors. Some were strong and sharp, others were not so strong, but all of them cloying and medicinal. My eyes were closed and I hated to open them... *'Those Odors'*... I wrinkled my nose. *'Aaagh! Ammonia,'* I brushed the hand away irritably and opened my eyes. I saw Alex's face fleetingly, then, a bespectacled, slight figure bent over the padded table on which I lay. Rheumy, blue eyes squinted and the spectacles were adjusted farther down on the boney nose. Snow white shaggy hair surrounded a cadaverous leathery face. There was a grunt, then a satisfied,

"Aaaah!" The young lady has some bruises and a cut on her arm, but she's goin' to be just fine! Got the wind knocked out'a her," he added. Doctor Morgan removed the stethoscope from around his scrawny neck and nodded to Alex. I suddenly noticed that poor Alex was holding his arm. He stepped forward.

"I'm sorry that I had to knock you down so hard, Miss, Rhyman. There wasn't time for anything else." Alex's smile held a hint of pain in their green depths. Dr. Morgan interrupted before I could say anything.

"Set ye'self down over here, young feller, so's ah kin have ah look it thet arm!"

He probed and prodded. Alex's yelp of pain brought me bolt upright.

"Broke, she is!" the doctor ruminated. "Gotta put ah splint on er' an' fix up some plaster fer ah cast." The doctor pointed toward me. "Look at the purdy young lady, she's ah settin up." Alex yelped again and his face grew ashen. I came down from the table with alacrity despite my aches and pains.

"Oh Alex, I am so sorry, your poor arm!" I brushed a wisp of the blonde hair back from his eyes. Sweat beaded his brow.

"You saved my life!" I looked into the green eyes. They grew dark and fathomless. He tossed his head and laughed,

"Ah shucks, ma'am", his exaggerated rejoinder imitated a southerner's draw perfectly. "T'wasn't nothing, sho nuff, coase, if you all was to decide to throw yo'self at mah feet, ah'd be obliged to ask you all ta dinnah!" he smiled that smile again. I giggled, pretending to fall prostrate before him. "Ah take it that yo-all accept, ma'am?" I cuffed his ear playfully.

"Since I owe you my life, I supposed it does."

"Well!" He smugly returned, "Yo-all may not be able to pay the debt with just one dinnah, ma'am. It might take any numbah of occasions of yoah pleasant company!" I stood up.

"Well, sir, you have asked for it! But be forewarned. There are those that say differently about my company!"

The rest of my day was spent purchasing, ordering and selecting the endless items for restoration of Claibourne plantation. I was very happily shopping when Jefferson made his appearance.

"A very good day to yo', mistruss, ah sho am glad to see yo' safe an' sound. Word wuz gwine roun' on de street 'bout a red haired lady gittin' run down by a freight waygon! Ah' sho is glad t'werent yo, Miss. Ah' wuz like to 'bein scaled tuh death!"

"Oh, but it was me, Jefferson. I was saved from injury by my new attorney Alex Robbins. I am very sad to say that the young man suffered a broken arm in doing so." I sighed.

"Oh lawd, Mistress Rhyman, ah shouldna run off down to de stables like ah done!" Jefferson lamented.

"Do not worry or say anymore about it, Jefferson. It was not your fault! I fear that I have been so busy purchasing that I completely forgot that we need better transportation. We shall retire immediately to the carriage house! Then to the stables! Although I doubt a proper team may be purchased here in town."

Just as I finished speaking, the manager of the store approached with my packages.

"Heah's yoah packages, Miss Rhyman. We shuah' do appreciate yoah patronage, an' is theah anything else we can do foah yo' today?" Before I could answer, the store keeper noticed Jefferson's presence.

"H'eah! Niggah! Whets the likes o' yo' doin in heah! Ya'll git out o' heah!" He looked at me apologetically spreading his hands. "Ah'm so sorry, ma'am, was he bothin' yo? Evah since that fellow Lincoln told 'em they uz free, they been gittin' uppity!" Jefferson had started for the door but I called him back.

"Jefferson! Come here!" Jefferson turned and stalked back into the store and stood by my side. The store keeper was perplexed.

"My deah Miss Rhyman, do yo-all know this niggah? I'm sorry, ah was not awayah that he belonged to yo' ma'am. Please accept my apologies." I speared the lil upstart with as cold a gaze as I could muster.

"It is not me that you owe an apology to sir, it is Jefferson. He is a free man, and a well employed one! He works for me and if I were you, I would treat a person of his means like a human being." I quoted Jeffersons salary. Jefferson's mouth fell open. His eyes bulged. He opened his mouth to protest, but I interrupted him.

"Be quiet, Jefferson! I turned to the store owner again. "I wish it to be known in Columbia, sir, that anyone who is in my employ will be treated in the same courteous, decent demeanor as I should expect to be treated! If I should hear of anyone not doing so, I shall bring to bear all the means at my disposal, sir, to put them out of business! If I may so, my means are quite formidable!" Jefferson's bulging eyes see-sawed back and forth from the store man to me. The proprietor looked at me with resentment in his eyes.

"My dear Miss Rhyman, you foaget yoah self! This is my property, an ah' do believe thet ah hay-ve the right to say who may be served oah allowed to entah mah premises!" He folded his arms.

"Of course, sir, I quite agree. May I ask how you obtain your merchandise?" I demurred.

"Like everyone else in this heah town. Ah ordah wholesale from up noath. Why do yo ask?" He guardedly eyed me with disdain.

"And how is it delivered to you, sir?" I queried.

"Why, by the railroad, of coase, ma'am," He quizzickly reported.

"And is this how everyone in Columbia receives their goods?" My red hair started to bristle. He went for the bait.

"Why yes, I do believe so. Freight wagons are too slow and can't carry enough to be economical. We only use them foah single ordahs. And only if thea's no hurry." He was enjoying his role of male businessman, of acquainting me, a mere female, of the complex and difficult matters of business.

"Are yo' undah standin' me ma'am, ah really do not desiah to boah yo' with man-talk, ah always said, business if

47

foah men, and child bearin' foah the women!" I closed the trap.

"I own the railroad!" I smiled very demurely. He turned white. "And I do believe that my attorneys in Baltimore have purchased seventy-five percent of the stock in your bank of Columbia, sir, and, do believe that the bank, my bank, holds the mortgage to this, oh establishment of yours, does it not, sir?" He turned red.

"And shipping, sir, oh we must not forget the possibility of sea trade of course," Another trap.

He thought he was saved. The breath he had been holding issued forth long and hissingly.

"Oh, yes, thea is the sea trade yoah railroad is not our only recoase foah livelihood!"

"I own the controlling interest in eighty percent of the sea trade, sir. You have heard of my firm by the name of Rhyman & Sons?" His eyes compared to Jeffersons for size.

"Come Jefferson, we must hasten if I am to have a look at all the rest of the retail establishments that the bank is subsidizing. I greatly fear that some of them may be too poorly managed to meet their legal obligations." I turned.

"I really must apologize for bothering you, sir. I always said behind every really profitable business, there is a woman!"

Jefferson led me to the carriage shop just alongside the blacksmith's establishment. The buildings were open and roomy. Carriages were parked all along in orderly rows under the low roofed sheds. Some were as dilapidated as the one in which Jefferson and I were riding.

"Good evening, Miss." A man with a black beard and mutton chop sideburns stepped from a small wooden framed cubicle marked 'OFFICE.'

"May I be of assistance?" He looked at Jefferson. To

my surprise he reached out and clapped Jefferson on the back.

"Why hello again, Jeffrey, this is the second time today! Guess you must have your eye on somethin', eh?" Jefferson smiled at the man.

"Lo Bob. When is yo' gwin'ta staht wuk today? Yo' bruthah Eli done been shoein' hosses since daylight this mownin'!" Bob grinned.

"Now Jeffery, mind yo' mannahs, ya'll know somebody's gotta be the brains of the outfit!" He grew slightly less cheerful. "Coase, slow as business is it don't take much brains to handle it."

Jefferson introduced me to the man saying,

"Dis is mah new mistress. She done own Claibourne Manor now. She be Miss Kelly Rhyman from Baltimo'. Miss Rhyman, dis is Bob Nolan, an all that racket yo' heahin down yondeh by tha foage is bein' made by his brothah Eli. Doan take no notice ta Bob callin' me Jeffrey, he on'y calls me dat 'cause he laks me so much."

"Sure, Jeffrey," Bob grinned, "You are my right hand hoss picker."

I could hear a hammer clanging on an anvil with clear, ringing notes.

"I'm pleased to make your acquaintance, Miss Rhyman." Bob Nolan acknowledged with a bow. Then he spread his hands.

"There's plenty to choose from, ma'am. Like I said business is slow now because of the war. Of coase, if I know Jeffrey, he's already got his eye on somethin'."

I turned to Jefferson, "Do you, Jefferson? Have you found something, ah, suitable for Claibourne?" Jefferson turned without further delay and strode down the lines of carriages, surreys, and wagons, he went straight to a huge pair of iron strapped oak doors in the back of the blacksmith shop. He threw the latch and stepped back.

"Thea she is, missy, tha finest in this heah town. And ain'nevah been none finah, even befo' th' wah, foah sho'!"

Dark tufted leather seats shone in the dim interior of the shed. Glossy yellow wheels capped with silver hubs set off the black and burgundy painted conveyance. It most certainly was the finest carriage that I had ever seen. Solid oak and mahogany trim graced the curved sides and the little half doors. Bright silver foot pedestals underneath the doors matched the silver hubs and the top supports.

"Ain' she a beauty now, Miss Rhyman, ya'll said the finest, an' ah dun foun' er, now, sho' nuff!" Jefferson rushed around pointing out the carriages fine points. Bob Nolan spoke softly.

"There's none like her, even in Charleston. I don't know why we kept her, should've sold her long ago. Heaven knows we need the money. I guess I just didn't want to see such a fine lady like her used commonly, none o' these, sorry, no-account, speculators. She's the spirit of the South to me, an' I don't want to see her spoiled! Coarse, ain't too many buyers been askin'." He turned to me.

"Yo' serious, ma'am bout this?" I looked at the carriage.

"Quite serious, sir, of course, I will pay a fair price, but not an exorbitant one. How much sir, are you asking?" Bob quoted a ridiculously low price. I looked at the man.

"Mr. Nolan, I said a fair price, sir," And quoted a figure much higher but still fair. "Now if this is acceptable to you, I shall give you a draft on the bank right now." Bob Nolan beamed.

"It sho' nuff is pleasin' to me, ma'am. An' if theah is anythin' else ah can do for yo' please ask."

"I need a most suitable team for the carriage, sir. I

50

wonder if you could help me with procuring them. Do you know if there are any available?" Bob rubbed his chin thoughtfully,

"No-oo, all the best hosses were taken by the army long ago. Only one team good enough left around here. They belong to Sam Puckett, pair o' matched bays. I believe that they belonged to Colonel Claibourne before. That's why they weren't snatched up by the cavalry." I smiled,

"Then perhaps we should call upon Mr. Puckett, sir." Jefferson please do go and inform Mr. Puckett that I wish to see him on, some urgent business. I shall wait upon the gentleman in Mr. Nolan's office."

Mr. Puckett arrived shortly thereafter. I was quite successful in acquiring his team in return for two of our pitiful horses and a sum that I am afraid astounded the poor man. I also purchased suitable harness and tack to match the carriage. Jefferson looked quite resplendent in his new coachman's uniform. He absolutely strutted.

"Sho, an' won't Callie's eyes bug out when we git's home!" New provisions and food stuffs ordered, I bid Jefferson goodnight until tomorrow. I had a dinner date!

8

~Between the Glade and the Ball~

Days passed into weeks, work on Claibourne Manor progressed very rapidly. When the bills began arriving in Baltimore, Franklin fired off a telegram which arrived to me on a beautiful, sunlit, dewy morning in September. A courier from Columbia brought it a day after it arrived over the wires. After paying the young man, I opened the envelope.

'Have you lost your mind-STOP-Coming immediately-STOP-attorneys advise sale of property-STOP-discontinue spending-STOP
STOP
Franklin Rhyman, ESQ.....'

I walked slowly along the path to the cemetery. Lately I found myself drifting in that direction, often for some unexplained reason. Of course, since the cemetery was on an elevated knoll it made it more possible to see how the work on the house was going. It was also one of the more beautiful spots on the plantation. The oaks there shadowed the moss and fern bordered opening. The little glade was peaceful. Somehow I could feel a soft, tranquillness that soothed and comforted deep within me. I touched the warm stones beside the colorful flowers.

'Fresh flowers, someone, Lucas,' I looked all around. No, he was gone! The little glade was deserted. Suddenly, I

felt depressed, as if a cloud had covered the sun. I stepped closer to the crypt. I traced the cut letters forever engraved upon the plaque.

'Alicia June,' Lucas's mother, 'I wonder what she thinks about what I am doing to her home? Would she approve?'

"Oh, Mom," I said aloud, "I do hope you approve of what I'm doing. I do so want it to be perfect. To be like it was before." Now why did I call her mom? My mother was dead.

Hot tears coursed down my cheeks as I lay my head against the unfeeling stone. I sobbed uncontrollably. Dad, Mom, my brothers! I had so little family left! There was no comfort in the little glade today. All the pent up feelings of loneliness burst forth from my heart in spasms of uncontrollable grief.

"Heah now, Miss Rhyman," A low soft voice murmured like water over stones. "Ya'll cryin like yo' heart is breakin', Sho, now, dahlin." I lifted a wet tear stained face to find Lucas's eyes gazing warmly into mine.

He reached out his arms and smiled! I stared dumbly, I then plunged, 'oh for shame,' right into his arms and against his chest. I continued to cry but only between exchanged smiles and warm gazing. Finally, when I realized that his lips were brushing my hair in soft comforting kisses did I regain my senses,

"Oh? Mr. Claibourne! I, I'm so sorry! I did not mean, oh please!" Lucas smiled, but this time there was no sarcasm mixed into the gesture.

"S'alright, Miss Rhyman. Doan' yo worry about it. Ah' nevah kiss an' tell!" he grinned.

"Oh, I did not kiss you, sir!" I objected.

"Why no, ma'am, yo' sho'ly did not. T'was I kissed yo!

Aftah seein' how yo aiyah fixin' up tha old place, how could I keep from it? Coase, it might be thet ah just could'nt stand to see such a sweet young lady cryin' so. Ah'm sorry, ah did, ma'am, an' ah am not apologizin' foah mah actions!" He looked at me searchingly. "Sho, an' maybe yo are sorry, seein as how ya'll are ah Yankee an' I'm ah Southunah?"

I heard myself objecting to his implied prejudice upon my part.

"But it wasn't really a kiss, was it Mr. Claibourne, just a small comforting gesture?" Lucas's black eyes bored into mine.

"Well an' what if it was real an' really on puhpose, like this!" He crushed his mouth to mine. A slow, numbing fire coursed through my veins, growing in heat until my soul and body was throbbing in deep drum like thundering of my heart. The kiss only ended when we both had to take a breath.

"Oh, my," I breathed. Lucas brushed an unruly curl from his eyes. I noticed that his hand trembled. "Lucas," I breathed softly. He dropped his eyes. "You forget yourself, sir." He looked away.

"Yes, I sho'ly did, ah beg yoah pahdon!" He turned to me entreatingly. "But ah meant no insult to yo', Miss Rhyman, ah just felt...uh...compelled, ma'am."

"I know," I murmured, "and no offense taken." I brushed that unruly curl from his forehead again with soft fingers.

"Because," I paused.

"Because what, ma'am?" Lucas' voice was low and vibrant.

"Because, I felt the same way," I answered truthfully. His eyes magnetized mine. I don't remember when the second kiss began, its memory merged into the confusion of many more being born, then dying to allow the rebirth of another.

Our love lifted and flared in oddly spaced trysts during

September. Culminating in October when I invited him to the future ball at Claibourne Manson. Franklin had arrived, and I had struggled to convince him there was no profit in selling the old mansion in such a poor condition as it had been. He slowly began to see the full potential of Claibourne Manor as an investment.

The first of my horses arrived, and Jefferson was like a boy in a candy shop. Still, I was hard pressed to find time for Lucas, and our little glade away from the world. *'How would Franklin react?'* he had never met Lucas Claibourne.

Lucas and I spent our fleeting time together talking of our lost loved ones, hopes, and dreams. We laughed and cried together. He still limped, and I sent telegrams inquiring from doctors up north concerning his wound, without his knowledge, of course. His southern pride would not endure accepting charity, I knew. Replies varied from hopeless diagnosis to glowing confidence of recovery.

The day of the ball had arrived, and I was greatly pleased and satisfied. The grand old lady of the south, Claibourne Manor, was reborn! The tables shone in candlelight, awaiting the groaning burdens of food soon to be placed upon their surfaces. The garden was resplendent, with the rushing, beautiful fawn fountain. Music played softly. Waltzes, ballads, and classics poured elegantly from violin, cello, and flute. My guests were arriving. My dream was realized and I was in love! Yes, my dream in southern velvet, Claibourne Manor Plantation, and.....Lucas! Such Happiness!

I was bursting with joy. Franklin and I greeted our guests with what I hoped was warm southern hospitality. Together, we met some of the old southern families who were a bit nervous at first and distrusting. The gentlemen were gracious and very chivalrous. Their wives, I'm afraid, were a bit cold in their manner. They stopped their simpering chatter immediately when I approached. Although, I spoke to each in turn trying to be quite social, they never really resumed their conversation until I was well on my way to another group of guests. I definitely detected a few, *'behind the hand,'* whispers as I passed by. *'What were they saying?'* I thought.

I stopped by the kitchen. The food was well prepared and the meal went wonderfully. The cooks had done an excellent job but only a temporary one. I still had been unable to secure a full time cook, unfortunately. Teresa Baynes came with a young man who clearly was quite younger than her. She obviously had not forgave me for the *'snake'* episode. Her curtsy of greeting was hardly a curtsy at all. Her manner was stilted and cold. To my chagrin, I observed Franklin talking quite animatedly with her.

Banker Hansen stood talking business with some well dressed gentleman from Columbia. My invitations to the ball had been generously broadcast in town. In such a case, you were bound to contract with some who were perhaps, non conformists. If I were not mistaken, these men were what the local gentry referred to as *'speculators'*. A better description described them as "carpet baggers", land grabbers who took advantage of the unfortunate people who had lost all but their land in the war. They paid ridiculously low prices, knowing that most of the people were desperate for clothes and food. If this did not work, some underhandedly paid the back taxes due on the land. Later, the owners were evicted due to the delinquent debt. In a word, they were crooks!

Mr. Hansen waved a pudgy, many ringed hand. I did not trust him and decided that I should look into his dealings now that Rhyman and Son's had gained control of the principle stock of the bank.

"Oh, there you are, Miss Rhyman, don't you look ravishing tonight. That is a most beautiful gown you are

56

wearing, and that necklace! It surely is quite obviously diamonds, is it not?"

The banker's glittery eyes took in all. My gown was a light, shimmering emerald silk from Paris. In fact, everything that I was wearing was imported. My slippers also were from Paris, the necklace, from England, my scarf of silk, from the Orient. Father had loved to purchase expensive gifts when abroad. We never knew what to expect from him. My gown, I hoped, matched my green eyes. His honor cleared his throat.

"My dear, you have certainly done wonders with this old monstrosity! However, I understand that it has incurred quite some expenditure on your part. Now I wonder if you might consider, er, selling? I am sure that you realize at this time, the great expense of maintaining such a place as this. I have a gentleman now who is prepared to make an offer. Of course, with prices down the way they are, you cannot hope to recoup all your losses and expenditures. I am afraid that there is not a great demand for such a place, the economy, of course." He waited, expectantly.

"Claibourne Manor is not for sale!" I stated firmly. His honor blustered.

"My dear young lady, think what you do! It is not everyone who has the means to purchase such a tract! I would strongly advise you to accept!"

I looked him in the eye. "Claibourne Manor is not for sale! Now if you'll excuse me..."

But your brother, Franklin, is it not? Gave me to understand that it was!" his honor grasped me by the arm.

"The lady does not wish to sell, Hansen! An' ah do believe she asked to be excused, Suh!" Banker Hansen glared then turned huffily away.

"Lucas! Where have you been?" I asked as Lucas, still eyeing Hansen, guided me away from the group.

"Dinner, I'm afraid is over. I thought you were not coming." I accused and Lucas smiled. He was very handsome in his tuxedo. It set off his very black eyes. I again had the feeling of familiarity. Where had I seen those eyes before? Oh well, it was just a feeling.

"Ah did not come to eat, Miss Rhyman, ah came to dance!" Smiling, he led me into the swirling, rushing throng, then, we began a dizzying, wonderful, kaleidoscope of dreamland ecstasy. I had always loved to dance. The music drowned out all sense of time and space. Although Lucas limped, he still did very well, and I was proud of him.

"Sho but the thought of some o' these others gentlemen getting' to dance with yo', an holdin' yo' overcomes any feah o' my handicap ma'am. Or any possible public humiliation thet might be incurred, Dahlin." I laughed.

"Could it be that you are jealous?"

"Coase not, just pu'ah selfishness on mah paht, dahlin." Teresa Baynes eyes were glowing pools of indignation. She kept turning her head around that of her partner, trying to follow Lucas and I through the swirling couples.

The look of hidden pain in Lucas' eyes brought me to my senses. I pretended to be tired and led him to a seat. As we talked, Alex Robbins approached.

"Good evening, Miss Rhyman, may I have this dance?" He smiled and extended his arm.

"So," I chided taking his arm, "another late comer. Do you have an invitation, sir, or did you decide to crash the party?" Alex laughed.

"I've been away. I only got back in a couple of hours ago. I heard about it in town, so here I am. Better late than never, you know." I smiled,

"Sure you are in the right place, you're new around here, you know."

"Everybody knows you're a Yankee." Alex grinned. "Of course, and so are you. You know, Miss Rhyman, we will always be Yankees to them."

Changing the subject I informed him,

"Alex, before you leave tonight I have a letter of instruction directing you of some legal requirements that I need." He feigned a shock.

"Miss Rhyman, discussing business on a night like this! You've just broken my heart!"

"I promise not to bother you about business again tonight." I apologized. Alex was a very good dancer. I turned to find Lucas had disappeared. Alex wanted to dance again, but I excused myself and went outside for a breath of fresh air.

It was a beautiful night. Couples walked in the garden and stopped to admire the fountain. It's musical, liquid song bubbled and trilled, the stone fawn stretched forth its neck for a drink. The child poured the water into the large pond as it reflected the stars and moon. A most beautiful full moon, its generous light illuminating and chasing shadows under the trees. I listened to the music, sipping at the glass of mint julep I held. I found myself at the wrought iron gate to the cemetery. *'Habit,'* I told myself. I opened the gate. I saw shadows move in the glade under the oaks. Then I heard Lucas' voice,

"Teresa! Foah God's sake!" A flurry of footsteps rushed down the path toward me. I quickly stepped aside into the shadows. The figure ran directly through the open gate. A scream rent the night. Teresa Baynes in a disheveled, torn bodice screamed again and ran directly toward the main house. I could hear her cries of,

"Help! Please help me!"

As soon as she entered the building, the music ceased.

I could hear a great hubbub, then shouts of anger. In the few moments of Teresa's flight, another figure came down the path of stepping stones. I couldn't see or recognize the dark shadows face, but I recognized the limp. Lucas!

In moments a group of men led by my brother Franklin came up the garden path. Farther back, the female gender of my guests followed. I stood where I was. Lucas stood beneath the oaks, waiting. He cursed to himself.

"Spiteful..." The men arrived, surrounding Lucas. Teresa burst through the ranks. She stood before them shamelessly, torn bodice hanging.

"There he is! That's the man!" She collapsed sobbing.

"He tried to take advantage of me!"

I stood in the shadows dumbstruck. *'Lucas, a rapist?'* Somehow in Teresa's case, I doubted if he would have had to. Alex Robbin's voice challenged Lucas.

"What have you to say for yourself, sir?" Lucas' voice came softly uncowed.

"Say, sir, why should I say anything? The lady has done all the talking. I only say one word!"

"And what is that, sir?" Alex's question came from his inevitable lawyer self.

"No!" Lucas' answer rang loud and clear into the night! "Liar," My brother Franklin hurled himself forward! There was a blow then another, and in horror, I saw Lucas hurled backward into the large oak tree behind him! He struck the tree with a crunch, and then collapsed. Franklin stood with fists clenched.

"Take that, sir!" He breathed heavily. Teresa laughed. Banker Hansen growled.

"Man ought a be horsewhipped!" Teresa laughed again hysterically.

9
~Matter of Decency and the Code~

Lucas struggled to rise, then fell back, groaning. He clutched his leg. The crowd gasped. The bone protruded from his bad leg in plain sight. One of the ladies fainted. I stepped forward from the shadows.

"Sis!" Franklin exclaimed. How long have you been standing there?"

"Long enough!" I lied fixing Teresa with an icy stare. Teresa gasped, then she spat defiantly at me.

"So! You're the one! I knew it! Lucas wouldn't tell me anything for sure! He threw me over for you! He was waiting for you!" I stepped closer to this cruel, spiteful person, sure now my hunch was right. I spoke softly so only she could hear.

"Teresa, remember the snake?" I put my hand in my pocket, suggestively. "Tell the truth!" I hissed. "Or I'm going to imagine that I see another, right there in your torn and ripped bodice!"

"You wouldn't dare!" Teresa didn't seem too confidant. Her eyes wavered.

"Yes!" I repeated, "A snake, right there in the bodice you tore yourself!" She blanched. "And remember, I love Lucas Claibourne!" Teresa looked carefully at my face.

"Alright, I don't care!" She repeated louder. "So, I lied! He jilted me! But I got even, didn't I!" She crowed. "Teach him a lesson, nobody says no to Teresa Baynes and gets away with it!" She picked up her skirts and fled down the path.

The disgusts in the men's faces were evident as she ran past them. Franklin's face went white with realization of what he had done. He looked at me with pleading eyes.

"Sis?"

I went to Lucas. The leg was crooked. The bone gleamed whitely. I fought back dizziness. Hot tears flooded my face. Lucas needed me now.

"Franklin, go get the doctor! Take the fastest horse we have." Franklin left quickly. Someone bring me some whiskey!" I cried. A flask was thrust into my hand. I tried to place the flask against his lips. He slapped it away violently.

"Let me alone! Ah, doan need any o' these Yankee cahpetbaggah's painkillah!" He shoved me away.

"Lucas!" he tried to rise again.

"Leavin, doan' nobody touch me again or ah'll kill yah, yah heah?" He shook his fist at the crowd. "Yankee hypocrites, all of yo!" He then passed out.

"Come on! Help me get him into the house!" The men hesitated,

"He said not to touch him," one of them mumbled.

"He was out of his mind from the pain! Come on help me for God's sake!" I made sure the poor leg was stationary. It seemed forever before we got him into the house. One of the men grumbled,

"Danged coward anyhow, 'taint wuth the bother." Another answered.

"I don't think so!" Alex Robbin's put in.

"He didn't run or back down out there. He stuck it out! I believe I know this man. If I'm right, he's a hell of a fighter and a hero."

Jefferson brought some laudanum from our medical supplies.

"Oh lawd, Miss Rhyman, Po Lucas, an' the bad laig, too!" he watched fretfully while I slipped the laudanum between Lucas' lips.

"He's out cold, Jefferson, but it's better that he doesn't wake up until Doctor Morgan gets here. It's going to be a while." I covered the bone with a warm, damp cloth. I'd read somewhere that you had to keep it moist. Jefferson looked at Lucas.

"Jus' look at em ah layin' thea, mistress, a body'd nevah know him fo wha'd he is, him a' sleepin like that. Oh lawd, theys gonna be hell ta pay!"

"What do you mean Jefferson? You know him for what he is. I demand you tell me!"

"Oh lawd, Miss Rhyman, hits jest...jes' that Marse Lucas, he... he gots an awful temper. Why he's killed five grown men in duels! Two of em' fer insultin' his ma, an' another three for other slights!" I stared at Jefferson shocked.

"Lucas, a killer, no, it could not be! Jefferson, are you beside yourself?" I looked at him angrily.

"Ain't no use, missy, but th'truth! Ol, J.C. had him ah temper, but t'wernt nothing to Lucas. Sometimes I b'lieve even his daddy was 'fraid o' him. But," Jefferson shook his head.

"Marse Lucas ain't no murderer. Evah one o' dem men had it comin' an' got it in ah stand up faih un'squayuh duel wi' gennulmen's rules! Ah loves him, mistress, ah couldn't be prouder o'no man! Cowahd! Sho'an' ain't it a good thing fer them men who said it, that Lucas Claibourne wuz out cold and couldn't heah!"

I protested, "But some men in town beat him up, you said so yourself! He didn't kill them did he?" Jefferson's eyes sparkled with fire! I could fully believe that he could be dangerous himself.

"Sho they did they beat him up, whole' bunch of 'em. Done what they al'us wanted to do but knowed they wasn't man 'nuff to do. In th' dark, so's he would'nt know who they wuz, the cowahds!"

Jefferson's fist smacked into his open palm with a crack like a pistol shot. Lucas moaned, I looked at his pain furrowed brow and mopped the seat away with a cool cloth.

"It'll be all right. I'll make it up to him. I'll make him forget!" Jefferson sighed,

"Yo loves him, don't yo', missy?" I nodded. "Guess Lucas loves yo' too, an awful lot!" My heart leaped.

Jefferson's mood darkened. His eyes held mine fiercely.

"Ya'll gonna halfta 'member that, Miss Rhyman. 'Cause all trouble is ah comin' an' yo' gotta lot to learn 'bout the south!" Jefferson's voice grew prophetically deep. "Dis is de south, not de no'th. An' some things ain' changed none! De law of honah amongst gennulemen is still in fo'ce even if' n hit is 'ginst th' law! Man gotta fight, else he nevah be able to live 'roun heah! Yo 'member ah said them duels wuz faih an' squa yah, ma'am?"

"Yes, I remember." I answered.

"Well, ma'am, yo' see them black eyes o' his'n, how could any man shoot straight w' them eyes a' lookin' back at him an'burnin' straight through his soul?" I shuddered at the thought. "Yo says yo loves Lucas, and ah hopes yo do cause it was yo' brodder Frank what called him ah liar an' hit him!" I leaped up from the bed.

"No! I will not permit such a thing! I shall make Franklin apologize and stand his medical expenses! Lucas will forgive him, if I ask him to!" Jefferson sighed.

"Like ah said, yo' got ah lot to learn, Miss Rhyman, Not meanin' no offence. But, apologizin', might work for th' insult o' the word liah, but t'wont wuk fer tha hittin! Das why gennulmen strikes each oddah wih' dey gloves, aftuh a blow is struck, on'y blood can pay th' debt! We'uns bettah pray, Miss Rhyman, an' pray haahd, foah eithuh way, no mattuh who wins, we'uns gonna lose somebody we loves!"

I had heard of the code, "Duello", many times before. Its legality had been revoked for only a short time, now. Widespread practice of the code had even once been accepted in New England society. It was clear that Lucas was the key to stopping such a senseless and tragic conflict. I had no doubt that I could handle Franklin. I looked at Lucas. Perhaps, he will not challenge Franklin.

'You're dreaming,' my common sense berated me. *'You heard from Jefferson about what Lucas is like. Perhaps they will miss. How stupid,'* Franklin most probably would miss, but not Lucas. He was most familiar with dueling pistols. Franklin had never been interested in firearms. His interest lay in more social pastimes.

'Face it, Kelly ol' girl, your brother hasn't a chance!' Oh my soul, in keeping Claibourne Manor had I signed my brother's death warrant? I loved them both!

It was silent in the old mansion. The only sound was the heavy, *'tick-tock'*, of the grandfather clock in the hall. Hours later I heard the doctor's buggy pull into the driveway. After making sure that Lucas was secure on this father's bed, I went downstairs. Jefferson was opening the door for the doctor at the end of the downstairs hall. Dr. Morgan's slight frame moved inside, followed closely by Franklin.

Franklin reached for the doctor's arm, thinking to usher him forward. Dr. Morgan shook it off, resentfully.

"Ah can fin' mah way upstay-ahs puhfectly well, thank yo' Suh," he looked at me through thick chipped spectacles.

"Good Evenin, Miss. Rhyman, whea's Lucas?" I replied

hoarsely,

"Upstairs in the Colonel's room." I hoped my tired red eyes did not show in the dim light of the hall. "Please hurry, doctor."

He shuffled down the hall and began ascending the stairs. Franklin tried to help with the Dr.'s bag.

"No Suh, no Suh, ah been doctorin' this heah fambley for yeah's, ol' Colonel and Miss June! Ah helped Miss June wi' the births o' all her boys, includin' Lucas! Day comes when ah can't carry mah bag ah'll jest quit doctorin'!" The doc fumed with indignation.

At last he reached the landing. I rushed forward to stand beside the bed. Dr. Morgan checked Lucas' pulse. He looked at the bottle of Laudanum on the table.

"How much?"

He squinted quizzickly at me as I told him.

"Good, you must give him exactly the same dosage every four hours. Well he's unconscious, so let's get the job done." Callie entered the room with a large pitcher of hot water.

"More," Doc Grunted. "Lots more!"

The doctor bathed the wound and the bone. Then he poured copious amounts of a strong-smelling disinfectant in and around the wound. Lucas stirred, groaning pitifully.

"We got to be quick." Doctor Morgan hissed. "Set th' bone, Jeffuhson, hold his shouldahs!" He looked at Franklin. "You too, Suh, Miss Rhyman, ah need you too. Help me with the leg. Ah'm not as strong as ah used to be! Easy, now, PULL!" I pulled.

"Harder!" The doctor ordered.

"Oh my no!" Lucas was coming to! Slowly the bone inched back into the raw, angry flesh. He moaned, turning his head from side to side.

"Oh, hurry! For God's sake, hurry!" I begged. Then

with a sucking, liquid sound the whitish protuberance disappeared. Doctor Morgan expertly straightened and set the bone with a twisting motion. Lucas cried out with pain and opened his eyes. The first thing he saw was Franklin.

"You! Ah'll kill yo'!"

The last word ended in a roar as from a lion. He tried to strike, but only caught hold of Franklin's wrist. Franklin's face grew red, and then white from what I could only believe was surprise, followed soon after by excruciating pain. The doctor's command was sharp and cut through my consciousness like a knife.

"Lucas! Cease and desist, Suh, this is yo' mothuh's house!" Lucas turned a pain filled face toward Dr. Morgan. I watched his face relax, he then saw me. He released his grip. Franklin stepped back, holding his wrist.

"The devil, the man has the strength of ten!" Lucas was bathed in sweat. His eyes drew mine as if they were magnets.

"Mistress Kelly Rhyman..." he said the words with a sarcasm that turned my heart to a quivering, jellied, inanimate object. His black eyes found Franklin again.

"Cahpet bagguh scum!" Lucas' anger was a living, seething terrifying flame. Doctor Morgan's long bony finger wavered and shook in Lucas' face.

"Lucas Claibourne! Yo' ah' th eldest son of Jaspuh Calhoun Claibourne! Yo' ah' th only one left of the Claibourne name! All o' yo' ancestuhs were gentlemen, Suh! Ah demand that yo' get yo'self in hand, and doan be the fust Claibourne to bring shame to yoah fambly name!"

Lucas' inner struggle with himself brought tears to my eyes. I could stand it no longer.

"Doctor if you are finished, sir, I ask that all of you please leave me alone with Mr. Claibourne. I must discuss matters with him if you please." Doctor Morgan, again, waved that boney finger attached to his boney arm.

"Ah must protest, madam, this man must have complete rest and quiet if he is to recover from his injury, absolute rest and quiet!"

"Of course, how thoughtless of me," I apologized.

"Perfectly alright, mistress," Doctor Morgan soothed quickly. He took a bottle from his bag. He thrust it to Lucas' lips.

"Drink Suh, s'good Kentucky Bourbon! You'll be needin' it!" He added, purposefully, while Lucas drank and then passed out.

10
~Searching~

My efforts to talk to Lucas were fruitless. In the days that followed, Lucas had few lucid moments. He would not talk to anyone. Sometimes I felt he was feigning sleep to escape talking to me. When I could no longer contain myself, I threw myself on the bed beside him and blurted out my fears of losing him. I kissed the feverish lips and shamelessly begged his forgiveness for my brother's hasty, shamefaced actions. I assured him of Franklin's remorseful apologies and that he was also suffering for being a gullible fool. Franklin, since that terrible night, had discovered that I was in love with Lucas.

"Oh Lord, sis," he had pleaded, "you don't know how much I've prayed that you'd found someone who would help you forget all the tragedy you've suffered over dad and our family. You were too cold and hard, too hard hit. I could see you hurting, but I couldn't get through to you, somehow, to loosen you up! Now you're in love with this, er' Lucas, and I've messed it up for you. I'll do anything to straighten this out."

He visibly blanched when I told him of the southerner's code of honor. I repeated Jefferson's words about Lucas' reputation of dueling.

"I can assure you, sis that I've no intention of shooting the man on top of wronging him the way I did. I shall simply refuse to duel, no matter what these Johnny-rebs say about it.

The devil! Imagine me in a duel? Not hardly! If I had it to do over, I'd think twice about taking him on again with my dukes, after feeling his grip!" He rubbed his wrist, reflectively. I knew Franklin was not a coward, and I was grateful for his willingness to atone. But my shameful outburst to Lucas brought no response.

"Oh wake up," I cried, "I know you can hear me! I know you're not asleep!" Lucas moaned and cried out deliriously,

"CHARGE! Up the hill, you Johnnie's, and give the blue bellied Yankees what for! Charge, I say!" His arm raised and fell as if swinging a saber. Guilt overwhelmed me. Lucas might die! I sent Jefferson for the Doctor Morgan. The Doctor found the wound infected, and had to reopen it for cleansing.

"Caught it in time maybe; and then again maybe not! Keep pourin' this on it." He instructed. "Keep tha flies away. He's gonna be a long time mendin, a year maybe."

Thee months later, Lucas left Claibourne Manor in the night without speaking to anyone. The door to his room stood open, but the bed was made up neatly. Callie and Jefferson denied any involvement with either the bed or Lucas' departure.

'What devilish pride,' a man with a still healing wound such as Lucas had sustained making his bed, resenting any help offered, no matter how much his enemy was indebted to him. 'Oh Lucas, Oh dear God please, please, help me to find him and to make him understand.'

I spent a lot of time either in the garden or the cemetery, hoping to catch Lucas tending the graves, but to no avail. Jefferson was the one tending them now. I questioned Jefferson as to Lucas' whereabouts, but Jefferson either would not say or did not know.

I then began riding everywhere on the plantation, and

to the cabin where Lucas had stayed. But the cabin was cold and empty, only a few of Lucas' meager belongings were left. I began to sleep fitfully, walking Claibourne Manor in the late hours, staring out the French doors at the garden and cemetery, drinking in the cool wind and shivering with the cold. My eyes constantly searched the night shadows of the hillside before me. *'There! Was that someone moving? There, in the moon glow between the oaks.'* I rushed downstairs and out into the brightly lit path to the cemetery. The gate stood open. Someone was here! *'Oh Lucas, Lucas, I love you so!'* I stopped, searching the dark shadows for my beloved. *'Oh where, where are you?'*

The moon beams did nothing toward warming the cold February wind. I shivered violently. I had only a nightgown on. In my haste, I had even forgotten my pistol. Then slowly, gracefully, a gossamer form appeared down the hill close to the stone crypt. It was there and then it was not. It faded in the darkness, and then slowly, ever so slowly it stepped directly into the bright moonshine. It was quite definitely a woman's form, but it moved soundlessly and airily toward the crypt. Slowly, she turned, looking directly toward me standing in the darkness of the oak behind me. She slowly lifted her arm and beckoned to me. *'It was Lucas's mother's ghost!'* My hair stood on end! Now all my shivering wasn't because of the cold. She stood still, beckoning, wanting me to follow her. *'Why?'* I wondered.

"Where," I stepped forward hesitantly. My question was answered promptly as soon as I started forward. I stopped, then started again as she turned and floated directly into the wide open door of the crypt! Did I dare follow? What could it mean? Was she angry with me over her son?

I swallowed hard, stepping gingerly up before the door of the crypt. I stared at the blackness and trembled. My hand

71

touched the cold stone. Then a hand reached suddenly out and jerked me forward. I screamed with terror again and again! Someone or something struck me on the back of the head and I fell down headlong into the blackness. I could hear the heavy, grating sound of the crypt door closing, and the bar being slid softly into place.

I came to after a while, how long, I don't know. I was lying on what felt to be crushed gravel, my head, touching a thick slab of stone. I felt nauseous and there was a tickling, sticky feeling on the back of my head and in my hair. I felt it oozing down my neck. *'Blood!'* I vaguely remembered being struck from behind. I felt tentively at the back of my head.

"Ouch, oooh," I suddenly remembered where I was! The crypt! How long? No light showed from anywhere. *'Of course! They build these things air tight, don't they?'* The dusty, cloying smell of decay was suddenly very noticeable.

I felt forward, my hand glided over stone, cold to the touch. The stone ended, and what felt like polished wood met my hand, *'The coffin!'* My terror mounted, and I suddenly realized how cold I was bone-cold, terribly cold. Shaking all over with chills, I realized I must get out!

I crawled toward where I thought the door might be only to bump painfully into the stone wall. The ceiling was low, so I could not stand fully upright. Forced to feel my way completely around the walls, I encountered polished wood twice, *'Lucas' mother and father!'* I was crazy with terror. I had to feel my way, inch by inch over the wood until it turned to stone again, then wood, then stone again. I felt my wound start to bleed. I was buried alive with two dead corpses,

"Help!" I shrieked, "Help!" At last I found the door. It was closed tight! I pushed with all my strength, but in vain. I screamed again. No use! *'If they build them airtight that means they're sound proof! I don't care I want out!'*

"Help, O' God, please help me! I screamed again.

"What was that?" I looked with horror-filled eyes as something began to glow against the back wall. *'There! Over the coffins!'* It got brighter and brighter. The eerie light was bluish green and I saw... Oh I saw, *'The Colonel!'* The same black eyes as I'd seen in the painting stared into mine. The lips moved, slowly to speak. A bony, thin finger was thrust toward me.

"Look well!" His voice was very faint. I could barely hear him speak. "Look well! You cannot let them find it! Look well! He must not find it! Look we-eelll..."

It was simply too much. The ghost came directly at me and I felt an even colder sensation at the instant of impact. But there was no solidness only a feeling that something cold as ice had passed directly through my soul. Oh how welcome the blessed embrace of deep, dark, oblivion!

11
~Ghosts or Reality~

'*I*'*m dreaming,*' I thought, *'This is too frightening to be real.'* I was cold, cold! I drifted in and out of consciousness. Shapes of vague forms moved and spoke to me. *'Father,'* My father was there before me! He smiled, and then suddenly, he changed, changed into the fiery old Colonel! The finger pointed, and then came the ghostly, dry voice,

"Look well-l..." Then there stood Lucas. He was silent and accusing. The black eyes gazed at me from a strangely wan and weak countenance. He leaned on the cane just gazing, gazing at me. Then, suddenly, we were kissing each other.

"Look well---ll" The Colonel was back! He was shaking me! I passed out again, and in a black mist, I seemed to hear Jefferson's voice calling me from far away. Irritating! The light was irritating! My head buzzed. I was dizzy. I put a hand up to shield my eye.

"Sis," Franklin sprang from a chair by the bed. "Sis, you're awake! Oh, thank God!" He bent over to kiss my forehead tenderly. "I thought that I had lost you."

"You almost did!" The voice of Doctor Morgan echoed hollowly in the room. "There," The old doctor finished closing the drapes over the French doors to my room, "better to keep light out of her eyes fo' a while, concussion," he added.

"And pneumonia!" put in Franklin. "I almost lost you,

and you're the only family I've got now! Dear sis." He bent and kissed my cheek. The hand that I tried to raise trembled and shook.

"It's alright, I know," Franklin's hand closed over mine. "I love you, too!"

Doctor Morgan's laudanum carried me away again to a soft, warm, so warm, sleep of contentment. I was going to be alright. My brother Franklin was here by my bed.

When next I awoke, Callie and Jefferson were moving busily about the room. I smelled fresh flowers. Beautiful sunlight streamed into the room. I heard birds singing through the open French doors.

"Good mawnin', mistress Rhyman." Jefferson's voice rumbled with pleasure. "Hit's sho nuff good to see ya'll with yo' eyes open agin. Close the door now Callie girl, we'uns done let 'nough air into the room, now." Callie smiled coyly, closing the French doors.

"Good morning, Jefferson. Oh please don't close the drapes!" I begged Callie. "I want to see the sun, see everything," I added.

"Yes, um" Callie answered.

"We gwine away now, mistress, and leave you to rest awhile." Jefferson shooed Callie out of the room and smiled at me from the door.

"Oh, Jefferson, where is my brother Franklin, please?" I had noticed the empty chair.

"Yo brother sho'nuff loves you, Miss Rhyman. He done set right daun there by your bed these heah long weeks, nigh onto a month an'ah half, right into May! Yo sho done been awfully sick, Missy. Some ladies come from town, but I run em off! Ol busy bodies ever one of em!" Jefferson's eyes blazed. Then he closed the door, leaving me to wonder and gazed dreamily out the French doors.

A red bird came to sit on the wrought iron of the balcony. He hopped about, his little eyes bright and searching. He flew down o the floor of the balcony. Immediately another bird lighted on the railing, *'His mate!'* I smiled.

'She's not as bright or as pretty,' I mused smiling. *'But he thinks she's beautiful!'* The red bird flitted up to sit beside his mate, and he lifted his bright tufted head to sing merrily.

"Oh I do want to get up, and go outside." I spoke aloud. "And I'm going to!"

"Oh no, you're not!" My brother stood in the door, "Not today, my dear sister." He strode to the bed to feel my brow, "No fever today, but you're not getting up just yet."

"Oh please, Franklin, please?" I smiled sweetly at him. Franklin softened visibly. Then he stood upright with his hand on his hips. "Not until the doc says you can." I dropped my head sadly. "C'mon now sis, I got to be careful for you now," he added seriously." If he says so, we'll get you up.

"Oh good," I thought to myself, determined to persuade the doctor any way I could. But Doctor Morgan proved quite impervious to my charming entreaties and also my temper.

"Don't work with me," he stated firmly. "I'm too old and I treated many a woman." He repacked his black bag. Franklin waited outside the door. The doctor paused after opening the door. Franklin stepped into the room. Doc Morgan looked at him and shook his finger at Franklin's nose.

"Only one hour, one hour a day at noon time! Warmest then," he added sternly and looked at me over his little spectacles, "One hour startin..." he paused teasing me. "Today!" he finished gleefully, and then he was gone down the hall to the staircase, his laughing, "he, he, he's," floating

76

back at me.

"The old imposter," I grinned, "too old huh!"

It was wonderful. I sipped hot chocolate and gazed rapturously from the balcony. Jefferson and Franklin had me smothered in blankets, though. I wanted to go down to the garden, but Jefferson stood guard quite dependably. His arms folded in real determination.

"No ma'am, one houh tha'sall an' that's that!"

But soon I was allowed two, then three hours. Tomorrow, I would go down and walk in the garden.

I woke early the next morning. I had dressed myself without Callie's help today. I sat over-looking the little knoll of the cemetery. There was the crypt! I shivered, thinking of the ordeal of terror that I had gone through. Had I really seen the ghosts? Or was I just hallucinating from the blow on the head? *'But I saw her, before I was struck!'* My matter-of-fact reasoning reminded me I wrinkled my brow in consideration. *'Why? Who? What reason?'*

Then I saw him. He was standing high on the knoll beside a large oak. From this vantage point, he could see through the French doors into my room if the drapes were open.

'Lucas', my heart leaped, *'my love!'* I stood up too quickly. I had to put out a hand to steady myself. He stepped forward involuntarily, and then as I had raised an outstretched hand towards him, he stood a moment gazing in my direction. Then with a wrench of his shoulders he turned and stepped from my sight.

"*Gone, He's gone!*" I stared with disbelief. *'How could he do this to me?'* I was becoming quite angry. *'He had said that he loved me! Why did he go away?'* I walked angrily back to my bedroom, closing the doors and even the drapes. I was so angry that I went downstairs. Franklin and Jefferson were defeated in short order.

"I will not go back into that room anymore except to sleep." I insisted. "Not another minute."

The next day, Doctor Morgan pronounced me perfectly well, but that I had to take everything a bit slower than usual.

"What's the matter, sis?" My brother probed, "Why are you mad at me?"

"It's not you. It's just that, well..."

"It's him, isn't it?" Franklin blazed. "You're thinking of him!"

"Yes, you are right, my dear brother, it is him. I saw him yesterday, on the knoll outside my room. I waved to him, and he just left! He turned away. Oh, I don't understand," I felt hot tears on my cheeks, I brushed them away."

"Well, I understand!" Franklin raged, "I understand the scoundrel! Remember the day that the sheriff came and questioned you? And you told us the whole story of the ghosts, the hit on the head, and someone locking you in the crypt? Oh I understand!" Franklin's eyes blazed. "And if I ever run into him, I'll..."

"But why? Why is it, Franklin dear please tell me what is the matter with you? Why do you hate him so? You wronged him, remember? Now why are you so angry with him?"

"The blaggard," Franklin strode back and forth across the room. "Do I dare tell you? Oh, I hate to tell you, you'll be hurt, even more now." He shook his head. "I didn't dare tell you while you were sick. I didn't think that rascal would have the nerve to return here. How wrong I was," Franklin growled.

"But what? Tell me, tell me now, Franklin!" I ordered firmly. "Ok, sis, I hope that you can take it, so, here goes."

"Do you remember the woman or ghost, or whatever it

was that you said you saw?"

"Yes," I added, "I did see her."

"Well, there was only one set of tracks outside the crypt door other than your own," he informed me angrily. "Not a women's tracks, but a man's tracks." He paused. "And beside those tracks were the marks of a cane!"

"No! I don't believe it!" I was dumbstruck.

"Yes! My dear sister, Lucas Claibourne, blaggard he is, is the one who attacked you!"

12
~Discovering Truth~

The joy of spring had no effect on me anymore. I didn't see the flowers, or hear the birds singing. The southern blue sky went unnoticed. Then the telegram arrived!

'My horses, my beloved horses,' I couldn't contain myself. I ran quickly down to the stables.

"Jefferson! The horses! My horses, the rest of them! They've arrived!" I was suddenly ashamed at my exuberance. Jefferson beamed.

"Sho now missy, that's the way I loves to see yo, now, happy! Yo, been grivin' yor'self ovah nothin', I reckon. Soons I hitch up the carriage, we un's will jus' go git us them horses. An on the way I gonna have a talk with Missy, yessah! Yo sho been grievin' yo'self fo nothin'."

Jefferson was ready almost as quickly as I, and we went down the road at a good clip, the fallow cotton fields interspersed with a few planted ones. There were new crops, but none that could compare with *'King Cotton'* in its heyday. No longer would ships depart Charleston with such cotton filled holds. Now, other cargo rode the swells across the ocean.

"Well, Jefferson, did you forget to talk to me or have you forgotten what it was you wanted to tell me?" I looked at him searchingly. Jefferson sighed,

"Sho' now, I'z reckon I wuz ah trying tah figgar on how to go 'bout it now. But here goes, straight on is the onliest way to git the job done."

"Well?" I pressed him, impatiently. I guess I know what he was going to say, and I was correct!

"Miss Rhyman, they done tol' you that t'was Lucas Claibourne what hurt you. But I know bettah, I promise yo' befo' de lawd dat t'wasn't him! Lucas didn't do it, no Suh! Aint no one dat mah Lucas hurt missy! He done love you, an' deys got tah be a nuthuh reason foah him bein' dere. I knows it!"

Jefferson looked at me straight and level.

"An iffin yo' loves him, yo' done knows it too!" I dropped my eyes before Jefferson's piercing scrutiny. Cowardly I avoided meeting his eyes. I did not know what to say. *'Oh, if it's only so,'* I hoped silently. Then I raised my head and looked at Jefferson.

"Uh, huh," Jefferson grinned gleefully. "Yo' done sho' nuff loves him, an' yo' knows it too! Ah kin see it in yo' eye, Missy, ah'm is satisfied! Now, les guan get dem hoss's. Ah caint haardly wait tuh set muh eyes on thet hossflesh! Hits gonna be likes the good ole times, befo' the wah! Cept," He added, "Without no 'count ole Dawkin's aroun', haw, haw, haw," Jefferson boomed out!

"Whoooo-ooeee! Look at dem dar hosses! Ah sear ah haint nevah seen the likes o' them. Cept once," Jefferson mused. "Jes' once, back befo' de wah, t'was Marse Lucas had him a hoss. Ah big black son of ah gun. But t'was real mean. Meanest hoss ever t'was, was dat hoss bit ol Colonel! Nobody could ride dis devil hoss, only Lucas! Marse Lucas went all de way to Baltimo' tag it dis hoss. He goes ta buy hosses, an' he comes back wid only one! Haw, haw, haw, Colonel, he done git real mad. He tries to put his hand on de black hoss, and gits bit fo tha tryin! Haw, haw, haint nevah been a hoss in da country like dis un. He dun hate evah body but Marse

Lucas and Marse Lucas loved dat hoss. Dat ole outlaw hoss loved him! He kill a man foah Lucas. An' Lucas kill foah him! De Yankees dey find dat out da hard way!"

'That was it!' I saw those black piercing eyes of the young man who dared step into the stall of my Pharaoh! I saw again that sure hand, the uncaring stance of the stranger before a raging black horse. He had stood taller, straighter, then. His clothing was fine, and his face much younger. I had not recognized him! But, the cane, the leg, the limp had all conspired to fool me! But I knew! I knew even before I asked the question of Jefferson.

"And what did he call this horse?" I stood very still, waiting.

"T'was good name foah this hoss, missy, dey was a king in Egypt-land dat treated de Lawd's peoples awful bad in de bible. Ah' mean king, a sho nuff, ah' mean king of hosses! His name was Pharaoh!" Jefferson sighed. "He gone now!"

"How, Jefferson? How did he die? I want to know, please." Tears filled my eyes, *'my Pharaoh!'*

"Tis a long story, missy, ah reckon hit'll have to wait till we gits headed home tomorrah. Too much to do now," He said apologetically. "We'z got to git dees hosses ready to head home, bright an early, 'bout daylight, I reckon, sho nuff." Oh I did not want to wait but realized that Jefferson was right. We had work to do!

Franklin was buying supplies from the mercantile. The wagon was filled to the brim with feed, tack, and other things.

"Here sis, have some horehound candy." Franklin thrust a bag into my hand. "I paid for a room at the hotel for you. Jefferson and I will have to stay with the horses, tonight, there's a lot of ruffians in town that would give their eye-teeth to have even one of our horses!"

"Sho nuff!" Jefferson agreed solemnly.

"But I want to stay here too!" I objected.

"Naw, missy, taint proper foah a lady tuh bed downs in de stables wid da men folks." Jefferson was wide eyed at the thought. No matter how hard I tried Jefferson and Franklin stuck to their guns.

"But they're my horses too!" I stormed.

"Our horses," Franklin corrected. "Now go on over to the hotel, we'll call you in the morning."

"Uhly in da mawnin," Jefferson grinned.

"Ok I know when I'm licked!" I laughed, and I set off for the hotel.

A good meal and a bath later, I was fast asleep. I guess I was still a little weak from the pneumonia. The next morning, I awoke to Franklin's laugh outside the door. He pounded harder on the door panels.

"Here now sis, are you dead in there? Rise and shine, sister, breakfast is served, and we got no time to lose!"

The hotel dining room was lit by smokey lamps with blackened glass chimneys. In the dim light, rough men sat eating hungrily. The walls were a faded rose pattern, once bright but now dingy and dilapidated. The food was very good, though. Bacon, biscuits' with gravy, and wild persimmon jam all put me into a festive mood. I should have to inquire as to the name of the cook.

Soon, we were on our way back to Claibourne. Franklin drove the wagon behind us. Our precious horses tied in a long line behind him. Each wore a strong halter, with a long, strong rope through the rings of each in turn. My horses had spirit, but they were well broken, all except one. He was the offspring of Pharaoh. Yes, Ramses was exactly like his father, mean, and hard to handle. He was still young though. He was the one on the end. Though he raged and pulled, the strength of the other horses before him drew him inexorably onward. There was no horse behind him to kick and if he rushed forward to bite, he was faced with a double set of heels. Soon, he settled down to jog sullenly along. But for now, he would wait his chance. Someone would pay for this indignity. The horse in front of him stayed well out of his reach, looking backward all the while so there would be no surprise attack.

"Sho' now, missy dat hoss look like de Pharaoh!"

"Does he?" I would lead Jefferson along, for a while.

"Speaking of Pharaoh, you promised to tell me about him and Lucas." I breathlessly waited the coming story of man and horse. When I sold Pharaoh, or lost him, to that black eyed young man, somehow I had known that the horse was loved and would no doubt be well cared for.

"Him, yessum, ah' gwine tell. Ah tell you of a grand hoss and his mastuh." Jefferson held me enthralled as he told me an incredible story of Lucas and Pharaoh.

Lucas had been an officer in the Confederate Calvary. He was a major with a huge black horse that no one else could ride. More than once men had paid with broken bones and injuries for trying to ride him. Lucas had fought one man for trying to shoot Pharaoh after being thrown and sorely injured. The man missed the horse in the dark, and was caught. The man had to be sent to the field hospital. Major Claibourne had fought at Bull Run, Shiloh, and finally Chattanooga. But it was in one of the small, unnamed skirmishes that Lucas received his wound. Twice decorated, the major and his horse gained notoriety and fame. The devil horse that could run down anything, they called Pharaoh, and could defeat most anything too.

The major's small contingent of Calvary was trotting across a meadow when the first shell of a fusillade of cannon fire burst directly in the middle of them. All were killed outright, or would die a short while later from their wounds. Except for Pharaoh, who was unscathed from the concussion of the blast, Lucas lay unconscious, his leg torn and bloody from a piece of shrapnel.

The Yankees charged with their own Calvary. Pharaoh met them head on before his master, according to the Yankee's own story of the incident. The black horse killed the officer in front, grabbing him off his horse by the neck and head. The huge teeth broke his neck and crushed the base of the skull. Then Pharaoh charged another rider, who went down before him. The horse trampled both to death.

"Shoot him! Shoot him!" A terrified sergeant yelled. "He's gonna kill me too!" Furiously spurring his own horse to escape the black fury, the sergeant was saved only by the pistols of his companions. Slowly the big horse sank to his knees, blood running from his nose. He snorted and screamed his anger and tried to rise, causing the men to fire again in fear.

Thus, did the horse that I had fed and nurtured, die valiantly. He defended his master to the end. Tears welled up in my eyes so that I couldn't see. I'm afraid that, tom-boy Kelly Rhyman sobbed very much like the woman that she actually was. *'Oh Pharaoh,'* I thought, "You great, black, wonderful horse!" Jefferson went on for a while.

"The major, now, he comes to in one of dem prison camps ob de Yankees, but he didn't 'member nothin'. He didn't know who he was or where he was from. He didn't even 'member his hoss. Dem Yankee doctors couldn't do nuthin 'foah his memberin', seems like. His leg healed all wrong too. Since dem Yankees didn't know his name, dey couldn't put it down on de list of de prisoners sent to de south. So evuh body figguhed thet since Lucas body wasn't where it supposed to be, wid da troop, he had done gone an' deserted. Some started callin him ah coward. Dey didn't know bout Pharaoh. It was over a half mile dat he had fought dem Yankee cavalry and he wuz killed dere behind some trees. So no hoss, no major. Dey figgered he had run away. Lucas didn't get hiz memory back until he met ah man who was a Sergeant in th' Yankee cavalry. H'it wuz nigh onto ah yeah aftuh the wah was ovuh. Dat sergeant told ah story 'bout a black hoss ah tryin' to kill him. An' dey shot de hoss to save him. Dey say Lucas went crazy mad. He beat dat sergeant, sum'n awful, and wuz dragged off ta jail foah thutty days."

"Lucas love foah dat hoss brought his 'memberin' back, I reckon. He searched out the place and buried what bones he could find an' put a stone there! Den he comes home, only he didn't have no home, no mo. Ol' Dawkins owned it. Shady thing dat! De Colonel wouldn't ta left dat place to dat po' white trash Dawkins! But banker Hansen swore to it, an showed a sworn affidavit to it. Said t'was just as good as ah' will, huh! So ol banker drawed up a new deed 'cause they couldn't find th' ol one!"

"And Dawkins gambled it away!" I finished the story."

"Jefferson," I teased, I had a horse, once, back home in Baltimore. The horse was black and mean. Nobody could ride him. Then one day a young man came to our stable. He was from South Carolina, and made me mad because he said that he could control the horse and I couldn't. So I bet him that if he couldn't he'd have to pay me double the price for my horse. And he accepted my wager. Just when I thought the horse would kill him for sure, the stupid horse began to whicker and follow him around the stall. I lost my horse to that young man from South Carolina!"

Jefferson stared, big-eyed and his mouth gaped open.

"Sho now miss, an' what wuz the name ob yo hoss,

pray tell?" I let him wait, pretending not to hear him. "Heah now, missy, yo can't be dat cruel to po Jefferson. Gwan an' tell me his name now."

"His name... was... Pharaoh!" I started to cry again. "Lawd have mercy," Jefferson swallowed hard. I think that he was about to cry also. "lawdy mercy!"

It was a full hour before either of us spoke again. Jefferson was the first.

"Den yo' done met Marse Lucas a'foah, Miss Rhyman, but why didn't yo let on, b'fo now?"

"I didn't recognize him, Jefferson. He had changed so much and now he seems much older, using a cane. I didn't know until you told me about his horse."

"Ah done see de han' of da Lawd in all of dis, missy! Sho nuff, you all wuz meant to be ah meetin each othuh now."

"Star crossed," I commented. "they call it being star crossed, fate!"

"Den dat hoss in de back of de string, dats why he reminds ole Jefferson of de Pharaoh?" He asked, looking at Ramses.

"Yes!" I agreed.

"Hallelujah! Won't Mars Lucas be pleased!" Jefferson gushed happily, "He done sho nuff be pleased now!"

This was the first definite indication that Jefferson did actually know Lucas's whereabouts. I was quite glad that Franklin had no way of overhearing Jefferson's words of a moment ago! The urge to question Jefferson was strong in me, but well did I know that this would be unite fruitless. Jefferson was very loyal to his former master. His convictions were also mine, no matter what Franklin said about the tracks found outside the crypt. We did not believe in Lucas's guilt. I could not believe that he would hurt me for any reason. Of course, as the saying goes, love is blind.

'Kelly, ol girl, Where Lucas is concerned you know you cannot be trusted to see well at all.' I was glad that the sheriff was unable to find him. Whatever the reason for his leaving, it was not he who had struck me, and locked me in the crypt!

Soon the Oakes of Claibourne came into sight.

"We-uns is home, missy. Sho nuff ah'm mighty glad, too! Hit' be best ta put des here hosses in they stalls foah awhile. So's dey kin git used to the idea thet they is southern hosses, now." Jefferson winked at me.

But where Ramses was concerned, we soon found out that his disposition was not noticeably improved. We got him into his stall only after he had severely bitten and kicked two of his stall mages. He was not always this unruly. Perhaps it was the strange stall.

"Sho, missy, an' this heah hoss gonna try ol' Jefferson's patience, he is! He jus lak his daddy, an' sho wish Lucas wuz heah ta he'p deal wid him, aint nevah seen ho hoss what didn't love dat man." He sighed, "But ah guess ol Jefferson got to 'member all de old tricks dat he use on Pharaoh, now. Still be some hot times 'roun' de stables, agin, haw, haw."

"Hey sis, dinner's served." Franklin strode up beaming. Lately, he had seemed not quite so happy to be here at Claibourne. I suspected the reason was the telegram that had arrived, announcing that we were to have the honor of his darling fiancé's presence very soon, tomorrow evening in fact.

Miss Evelyn Prentiss Burgoyne should arrive on the six o'clock train. She was quite lovely, but I still felt that she was getting the best of the bargain where Franklin was concerned. Of course, if my sweet brother had to have a wife, she was the best of all the young ladies in Baltimore. Hers was an old family, high on the social scales. She had had many suitors, but she had said yes to my dear brother's proposal of marriage.

Dinner was not so bad, this time. Callie seemed to be making progress in her culinary talents after all. We all retired early, for we were very exhausted from our little trip to Columbia. Franklin was visibly in high spirits. Despite his exuberance, it was he who retired first to dream of his sweetheart, I suppose.

After a long soak in hot, sweet scented bathwater, I snuggled deep into the pre-warmed blankets and coverlets. Soft, downy pillows cradled my head. Behind closed eyelids, I saw the black sparkling eyes again. Lucas was never out of my mind for long anymore. Tonight, he came to me again, his smile for me warm and yet, intriguing. Lucas my beloved....

13

~Of Shadows and Horses~

The wonderful, beautiful sounds of a Southern morning in late spring brought me to a delicious, warm awakening. Mr. Red bird hopped about the balcony railing. Every little bit he would stop and stare at my bed with his little, black, beady, eyes. Now he lifted his small head in song. I could smell the sweet, varied perfumes of the flower garden on the warm breeze.

Callie had opened the doors to the balcony as usual. I loved it. I loved this beautiful, warm land of the South. I could hear the whinnying of the horses down at the stables. I slowly moved my gaze around the room. The furniture was a deep rich mahogany except for the four poster bed that I lay in. The bed was of ebony and teak. The posts were capped with ivory. Spiral rings went round and round to the top of the posts, where the powder-blue of the ruffled top gave the illusion of a blue sky. The beveled glass of the mirrored dresser reflected the gold, blue, and rose pattern of the textured walls. A crystal vase held daffodils, their yellow sunshine glowing in the morning light. *'Oh, it was all too lovely, too colorful to remain in bed!'* I dressed hurriedly and went downstairs after standing on the balcony breathing in the heady air of Claibourne.

I saw no sign of Jefferson. Callie smiled at me and placed a wonderful breakfast of corn-pone cakes with maple syrup before me. Eggs and bacon followed. I drank black coffee, but refused the ever present grits. I was not quite that

Southern yet! Miss Kelly Rhyman had always been an out-of-doors type of female. My father, I supposed, had a lot to do with indoctrinating me with the outdoor life. I loved to fish, and ride my wonderful horses. I simply must get outside!

The morning sun was warm on my shoulders. I had not hired a gardener, even though I knew that I must. I had done most of the work, but there was a lot left to be done. I tore myself away from the garden to walk down to the stables. Sweet smelling hay filled the mangers and my darling horses munched contentedly.

"Oh, theah yo is, missy," Jefferson greeted me with one of his dazzling smiles. "sho aint she a beautiful mawnin! H'it done sho nuff makes ah man glad to be alive now." He curried and brushed a bay mare that we called Sheba. Sheba was the dam of Ramses. Usually gentle in nature, never the less she had a temper if aroused. But her tempers were rare, and she was one of my favorites. I noticed that Jefferson had a slight medicinal odor about him. He had a fresh bandage his right bicep!

"Awe' now, Miss Rhyman, h'its jes ah little ole bite now. Ramses done gone an' caught me bein' ah' lil careless. But ah reckons thet ah'm ah might rusty and out ah practice, fo'sho! We'uns gwina git along jus' fine, purdy soon now!" He moved away from my concerned endeavor to examine his wound.

"No, now, missy, ah done took cares of it now! Doan yo' worry. Gwan now, and let me gits back ta wuk. They's lots ta be done wi'all dees hosses heah, now." His protests against my assistance were cheerfully ignored.

I had always loved grooming my horses. Soon, all was finished. I leaned against Ramses' stall, admiring his shining, rippling coat as he pranced and snorted. He squealed and rushed around, then stopped to paw the straw covered floor of the stall. He wanted to go to the mares. Today, he would be turned out to the largest of the holding pens. This was a grassy paddock, more or less a small pasture. When the mares were ready, they would be turned into this domain. He would sire many colts for us, I was sure. The day was down to deep purple twilight in a very short time, too short for my desire.

The arrival of Evelyn threatened to happen with me still unwashed and undressed for the occasion. I hurried inside for a quick bath, and dressed in an emerald green chiffon dress, accented by matching slippers and an emerald necklace purchased for me by my late father. The necklace's stones were set in golden ovals encircled by small seed pearls.

Dinner was a resplendent affair. Apparently Franklin had requested that our best china, crystal and silver be used. But it was also late because a reasonable length of time had to be allowed for our illustrious traveler to refresh herself with a bath and a short rest.

Franklin was very attentive to Evelyn's every mood. It was quite amusing to see his boyish antics. Evelyn smiled graciously and sweetly, although I felt, perhaps, a bit reserved. Claibourne Manor had been very fine in the past, perhaps she found something a little rough. Maybe even Franklin's sister, the tomboy. I shook off the pettish thoughts and dismissed myself to the garden allowing the two love birds to be alone.

The moon was bright and full, it's soft, mellow glow sending soft beams over the marble fountain. The stone was cool to my touch. I slowly meandered along the garden path, lost in pleasant thought. It was such a beautiful night.

'That certainly is a lover's moon if Franklin only knew he would be taking advantage of the situation.' But it was good to have the night to myself. I loved walking in the moonlight. I turned toward the stables, crossing a silvery moonbeam, and then entered a patch of darkness under one of the large oak trees. I was standing and admiring the night. I laughed at the thought that I had seen the ghosts of Lucas' parents. Shivering, I crossly rebuked myself for believing in ghosts. Of course, it had to have been the blow to the head, so it all had only been hallucinations.

'Ghosts indeed, but someone had struck me,' remembering angrily. 'I definitely hadn't slipped or fallen and most certainly someone had barred the door from the outside! Oh but it could not have been Lucas! He loved me, and I loved him! But if it had not been Lucas, then who was it?' I knew of absolutely no one who wanted to kill me.

'Who was my enemy? Teresa Bates? Oh this is getting really absurd, now. Certainly, someone who was afraid of snakes and creatures would not be out wandering around at night. No, it could not have been Teresa.'

My mind was still pondering the problem when the shadow moved. He stood to the far end of the corral where Ramses was penned. 'Lucas,' I smiled. 'He had not been able to resist having a closer look at Ramses! Perhaps the horse was the key to getting him to come out of hiding! I most certainly would not press any charges against him, no matter what the sheriff and Franklin said.' He moved farther around the corral disappearing into the darkness of the stables. I moved swiftly after him. 'I should make him understand that everything would be alright, and convince him of my love and Franklin's regret.'

Walking faster, the sound of a horse munching oats shocked me into noticing the open corral gate. Ramses could have gotten out! I angrily walked into the corral to bring the gate around so that I could close it. Who had given Ramses oats? I had forbidden Jefferson to feed the horses except at definitely prescribed times! Irregularity in feeding could upset a horse's system.

I latched the gate and moved toward Ramses to take away the oats. The horse stopped eating and looked at me. His ears went back. But Ramses will not hurt me, I reminded myself. He was unruly, but he had never actually hurt me. Feigned bites and kicks were about all that he had ever threatened, and those only to show off. I knew that he really liked me, but not to the extent of loving me the way some horses love their masters.

"Whoa, now Ramses, easy now, it's just me," I spoke gently, still moving forward confidently. The ears pressed flatter against the horse's head, and I was shocked into immobility! His teeth flared savagely in the moonlight. He reared, pawing the air, and then dropped to all four feet. Then he came to me with a menacing, cat and mouse stalk. He held his head low. I could hear the grinding sounds of his teeth.

"Ramses!" *'He never acted in this manner! Why was he acting like a killer?'* I opened my mouth to scold him and the sound froze in my throat.

The stalk became a rush as I saw with terror-filled eyes that this was not Ramses! This horse was heavier, older! I turned to run but it was too late! I felt the searing pain of huge teeth scrunch into the muscles of my back, and then I was flung violently into the air, against the bars of the corral! I screamed as I was thrown down. My face hit one of the bars and I tasted blood. My lower lip had been bitten through by my own teeth on impact with the wooden rail of the fence. The horse struck at me as I lay under the fence. His huge fore hooves pawed and stomped. One of his legs caught over the lower rail or else I should surely have been brained. As it was, I received a cut scalp and lost some of my hair.

The horse screamed with fury, he was having trouble getting his foreleg loose from the lower rail. He lunged

94

backward and the rail broke in two with a loud crack. *'Now! Now he could kill me!'* He whirled away to come charging back, his teeth reaching for me. *'Those teeth could crush my skull!'* I screamed again in terror as certain death rushed upon me. Then there was a flash like as of lightning and the horse screamed again. He began to fall. The great body followed the savage head into the grass of the corral and started to somersault over. I could not move as the mass of trembling muscles and heavy flesh came over, then down, down, directly onto the poles above me. The poles shattered, and then his crushing weight drove the air from my lungs and the consciousness from my brain!

"She's going to be just fine, now" The voice of Doctor Morgan awakened me to a pain filled world. My whole body ached. "Nothing's broken, but she has severe lacerations and bruises. "The air was knocked out of her."

Jefferson stood over by the door. His eyes dropped, refusing to meet mine. His smile was gone, and he did not say a word. I looked again and saw the sheriff standing close by with another man, obviously a deputy.

"We'd like to ask Miss Rhyman some questions." Sheriff Abrams stepped closer, "if'n s'alright, doctor." He added, at Doctor Morgan's glare.

"Well," the doctor agreed reluctantly. "But just a few, questions, mind you now." He began to prepare a needle and syringe. It was quite obvious who the needle was for.

"My dear Miss Rhyman, this heah is the second time that you' all have come to grief, I see. The first time was the incident in the grave yahd, was it not?"

Sheriff Abrams was a balding, yet solid man. He had a handlebar mustache the color of straw accenting his long, hooked nose. The nose was red. I suspected from whiskey consumption. Heavy thick eyebrows overhung his watery blue eyes that were also bloodshot.

"Yes." My voice sounded strangely weak and high. The sheriff's right thumb was nervously picking at the handle of his revolver.

The deputy, a tall, slim man of rough appearance, looked bored.

"Can you tell me if there is anyone that yo' can think of, who would wish to er... get rid of yo' ma'am, other than this er..., Lucas Claibourne that you know of?"

"Why sheriff, Lucas Claibourne would no more hurt me than would er-uh Jefferson would, isn't that right, Jefferson?" I looked pleadingly at my groom.

Jefferson did not look up. His head was down and I could only see his mouth set in a straight hard line.

"Well, Ma'am, we know most of what has gone on heah. According to your groom, this was not you'alls hoss that attacked yo'. He says that this hoss was a stranger, a killer, obviously, by the way that he acted. He also says thet he doan know where this heah hoss come from! Is this right?"

"Yes." I agreed, "But we do have a black horse called Ramses who was supposed to be in that paddock."

"Well, he's not theah, Miss Rhyman. An' it do appeah that whoevah put this killah hoss in yo'paddock done up an' took yo'hoss in the bahgain. Yo' man Jeffuhson heah, says that they is also one of yo' saddles missing. Do yo' have any idea why Lucas Claibourne would do this, ma'am?"

"Why no, I have no idea unless..."

"We already know about your brothers little set to with this Lucas fellow, Ma'am. Did yo by any chance happen to see this er-party in question on the premises tonight? I mean when you wuh down at the stables, mebbie?"

"Well, yes, I believe that I did see him, but I don't see what that could prove, Sheriff after all...."

"Just a minute," Doctor Morgan interrupted. He took my arm in his grasp, I winced because the arm was dreadfully sore. The laudanum went down quickly. He apologized.

"Now," he said to the sheriff. "If'n yo got anymore questions, you better hurry. She'll be going to sleep, real soon now." He started to close his black bag.

"No more questions," Sheriff Abrams grunted. "I reckon her seein' this here Lucas clinches it! His boot tracks, Calvary boots at thet, are all over the place, just lihke thet night in the graveyard. Boot an' cane prints. I reckon he's the one, right enough! We'll get him, though, ah promise you that, Miss Rhyman, he's gonna pay fer all he's done. I reckon he'll hang, shore. Scarin' folks and lockin'em in tombs is one thing, but murder is another." He turned to leave. The doctor's laudanum was beginning to make me woozy.

"Murder?" I said thickly, "Whose murder? I was not killed! Why should you charge him with murder?" The sheriff looked at the doctor, who waved him on out of the room. Doctor Morgan moved to the head of my bed and looked at my eyes.

"I guess now is the best time to tell you, Miss Rhyman. Franklin, yoah brother, was outside in the garden with Miss Evelyn, when he heard yo' scream. He comes ah' runnin' an' shot that killer hoss thet wuz a tryin to kill yo'. That hoss fell on yo' and knocked yoah out or yoah might have seen who fiahed the second shot. Yo' brothah Franklin saved your life!"

"But who got killed?" I dreaded the answer. "Oh please, what are you trying to tell me doctor?"

"It's alright yoah' ll be asleep any minute, now." "Yoah've got to be told soonah uh latah, and I reckon now is best." He leaned over to me with gentle demeanor and placed his hand on mine. "Whoever put thet killah hoss in that corral

97

fi'ahed ah second shot! And," He dropped his head, "they shot yoah po' brothuh, Miss Rhyman!"

I wanted to scream, but I couldn't. The doctor knew his laudanum.

"Ahm so sorreh, my dear." His image faded away and my world whirled into darkness.

14
~Revenge Revelation~

The click-clack of the wheels against the iron rails beat a monotonous rhythm with my thoughts. *'Franklin dead, and I'm alone! Franklin dead, I'm alone! I'm the last of the Rhyman line! Oh Father! Oh dear Franklin! Oh I am so sorry! It's all my fault! If I hadn't insisted on staying in South Carolina, Franklin would still be alive! Oh dear God, please forgive me! Oh, dear Franklin! He had saved my life, and I had cost him his!'*

Now I was taking him to Baltimore. I could not bury him in South Carolina. He shall rest beside father and mother along with my two older brothers who were killed in the war.

Across the narrow aisle, Evelyn sat beside Alex Robbins who gave his attention alternately between two distraught, tearful females. Evelyn was softly weeping. Her beautiful face buried in Alex's handkerchief. High society or not, Evelyn had truly loved dear Franklin. I was glad when she finally collapsed into a much needed, merciful slumber.

After making her as comfortable as possible, Alex moved across the aisle to sit beside me. He said nothing, only looking at me with caring sympathy. We sat there together, staring out the window as the unseen scenery flowed by the passenger car windows. Tears filled my eyes as I thought of dear Franklin's coffin riding in the next car. *'Oh dear, how shall I ever survive the next few days, it's too hard?'*

The grief, sorrow, and guilt weighted so heavily on my

heart that I thought that it would stop under the heavy
burden. I was grateful for Alex's comfort and companionship,
through. According to him, he had been going to Baltimore on
business. I glanced away from the window to catch him
gazing at me with a wrinkled brow and concerned eyes.

"May I get you something from the dining car, Miss
Rhyman, something to drink, perhaps?" He smiled at me.

Alex Robbins was good looking, I decided. His
manners were very refined. You could tell that he must be
from a family of quality.

"Yes, please, if you don't mind, some coffee." I
managed a brief smile. "Black, if you please, and very hot!"

He stood up, grateful for the opportunity and the excuse
to stretch himself and move around. He tipped his hat,

"The lady's wish is my command!" Then he went out.
Very shortly he was back with two large mugs of black
coffee.

"Thank you, Alex, you are very kind. I do appreciate
your help and assistance, let me say. I don't know how I
should have managed without you. The arrangements and
all..." My voice trembled."

I only wish is for you to consider me anytime that you
need anything, Miss Rhyman, anything at all." And he added,
"Also, I do hope that we are to be very er-ah close friends,
my dear, Miss Rhyman." He patted my hand.

"We may not have the time, Mr. Robbins; I have
decided to sell Claibourne. I shall desire for you to handle the
circumstances, if you please. I am sure that you
understand..."

Alex stared at me after quite visibly stiffening his
demeanor.

"After the funeral," I shakily offered.

"Yes, after the funeral," he repeated. "Then I shall do

everything in my power to talk you out of it." He softened. "You cannot expect me to give up my very close friend so easily, so soon, do you my dear? After all, South Carolina needs you too much."

"South Carolina! She started the war! And, and she killed two of my brothers! And now, she's killed Franklin too! Oh how I hate her, I hate South Carolina! I wish that I had never come to South Carolina!"

I turned away to gaze out the window. Twilight was casting deep purple shadows over the landscape. Lights were twinkling in the little houses. Alex shifted uncomfortably,

"There, my dear, I am sorry. You have suffered some very heavy blows in life, I fear. But I promise you, everything will be alright very soon, I assure you." He sighed.

The wheels beat their way into my conscience again, *'clickity, clack, cliquey, clock. Franklin's gone, your alone, Franklin's dead, it's your fault'*... I stared into the darkness. The little single lonely lights shone out occasionally. They were just like me, all alone in the darkness.

Alex's presence was very much in evidence the next few days. He called at my former home. He sent flowers, he attended Franklin's funeral. He seemed to turn up everywhere even when I went to dinner alone. I barely sat down and there he was!

"My dear sir, do you not think it quite improper for me to be seen out on the town so soon after my brother's funeral? Alone I should be forgiven, but with a man present well, tongues will wag, you know." I smiled to take the sting from my words.

"But in times of grief, are not close friends expected to be in attendance, my dear? After all, one has to eat and I do intend to remain you very, very closest friend!" He grinned,

"Besides, I do not think that Kelly Rhyman cares a hoot about a lot of gossiping old hens. Not if you're at all like the girl that your father described to me."

"Oh, and did you know my father for any length of time, sir?"

"Yes, quite! He had me do a lot of ah... interesting deals. Quite an interesting man your father, always on top of things. He was nobody's fool. I never knew him to run from a fight. Alex, he would say, we're in to the bitter end. We'll fight to the finish! Hooray for the drink!"

I laughed. It sounded just like father. Yes he was, had been, a wonderful, battling, old Irish gentleman. I was proud of him, to be his daughter.

"But your business, my dear Alex, I thought that you had business. How could you find the time?"

"My dear Miss Rhyman, you are my business, and shall be for quite some time to come. Here's to the Irish ladies, hoorah, and to Kelly Rhyman, who is blushing furiously just now, hoorah!"

"Oh, you are terrible, Alex Robbins, terrible! And... and, insufferable, and... and, thank you so much for being my friend!" I gratefully added.

"A very close friend from here on out," he smiled. I surrendered, "But you will be sorry for sometimes my friends find me a little hard to handle. I do have an Irish temper you know, and..."

"Red hair, also?" Alex's impish grin widened into a delightful laugh, "Now, now, we are in public my dear, and remember the wagging tongues? They most certainly would not approve of the way you are looking at me just now. Such fire, such flashy eyes, I do believe that you are about to throw your glass at me, I fear. And me, your very closest friend!" He pursed his lips chidingly.

"Mr. Robbins, there may very well be times that one is better off to be not so close, after all." I said with feigned crossness.

"Yes, I do believe that you are right," Alex smugly replied, "But a fire gives comfort as well as burns, does it not?"

We arrived back in Columbia just before nightfall. It was raining. The steady down pour of the rain on the roof of the hotel was somehow comforting. Alex had excused himself after our hurried meal in the dining room. He had invited me to breakfast, but I refused him gently. My body ached, and my mind throbbed with fatigue. I lay in bed, listening to the wonderful, cleansing rain.

'Tomorrow, I should arrive back at Claibourne, my wonderful old Claibourne. And now I must sell her... Oh what must I do? I was alone, sole heir to fathers beloved business interests. Yes, he had loved his business. He loved a good fight. What would he do now? Would he sell? Would he?' I thought of Lucas Claibourne, *'he who had taken my love and now had killed my poor Franklin.'*

It was true that Lucas had a justifiable reason to be angry, but to kill? And Franklin had tried to make amends. But the pride, the same terrible, foolish burning pride that kept South Carolina still undefeated in spirit, if not in body, this was Lucas's legacy. He had reminded me of father. But now he should discover that I am truly my father's daughter. I had the Irish blood and the temper to match! *'If Claibourne was to be sold, it would only be after my brother's killer was caught and hung for the dastardly deed that he had committed!'*

'A duel!' He had a reputation for dueling. "Fair and square," Jefferson had put it! Franklin had been given no chance, no requisite for reconciliation. He was shot down in

the dark like a dog! Murdered! If his murderer should again appear in my sight, he would find in me also a true marksman.

'*Oh, how I had misjudged him.*' Not often had I ever misjudged anyone so badly. Poor Franklin had paid for my mistake. Now, I will give myself to the capture and punishment of his killer. '*Tomorrow…. I shall hire a detective, Oh, I will…. I will….*' I grasped the glass figurine on the table and threw it into the fireplace. It shattered loudly.

"There! There's your love Kelly Rhyman! Shattered all in little bright shining pieces! Lucas Claibourne!" My voice smoked with grief, then burst into the red hot flame of anger! "Lucas Claibourne! I shall dedicate my life, sir, to making you pay!" I fell across the bed sobbing.

"Hey, what's going on in there?" There was a pounding on the door. The man's voice was followed by a woman's voice.

"Oh pay no attention, sweetie, it's just a lovers spat."

"But I thought I heard a woman cryin!" The male voice said. Their voices faded away as I dropped into a black exhausted sleep.

15
~Vengeful Exploration~

The next day dawned bright, breezy, and clear. The wind was cool and blustery, taking away the warmth of the sun. The horse's hooves splattered through the mud puddles, evidence of the rain the night before. Little rivulets gurgled on their merry way, searching for a larger, more boisterous stream. Claibourne Manor now seemed a far away dream.

I spent the entire day in my room. The French doors to the balcony were shut and the heavy curtains drawn. A pall of gloom seemed to settle over the old mansion. Not a sound broke the heavy, clogging stillness. I had not heard Callie or Jefferson so much as close a door, clatter a plate, or make any other sound of normal life. Even the animals were quiet. No birds sang, no chattering of a squirrel, or neighing of a horse. It seemed that life here was cursed. First Lucas's family and now mine.

Lucas's face and eyes floated before me. I realized with chagrin and shame that I had truly loved this man, Lucas Claibourne, this son of the south. The black eyes glowed with warmth and love, and then they turned fiery and angry. Frustration and anger moved me to throw open the curtains and the French doors. I stood with the cold wind blowing my red hair there on the balcony. My eyes searched the garden, the knoll, the cemetery.

'Oh, where are you? Where do you hide? You have betrayed me, Lucas!' I realized with a shiver that this man, this murderer, could be very close by. I fingered the little

pistol in my pocket. The little revolver was my present companion, now.

'Tomorrow,' I decided, 'Tomorrow, I shall explore Claibourne plantation right down to the last ree and stone.' I had a feeling, a crazy, unreasonable feeling that Lucas was close by. *'But he would be crazy to stick around, when he should be far away, running from the law.'* For some strange reason, I was more afraid that the latter was true and he was close by.

I had Jefferson bring supper to my room. I gave him instructions that early on the morrow he should send several careful worded telegrams to various detective agencies, including the Pinkerton Agency. *'If Lucas Claibourne could be found, I would find him,'* I vowed! The Rhyman name had far reaching connection. While others searched elsewhere, I should search Claibourne Plantation!

Rising early, I ate a quick breakfast and took a hot bath. I then, dressed in a riding skirt and jacket. After sending Callie to town with Jefferson, the freedom came to poke around everywhere. Jefferson would have no opportunity to warn Lucas if he were hiding at Claibourne! First, the barn! Lucas loved horses. It made sense. I'm afraid that I prowled and crept around the moldy stalls quite unladylike. The horses whickered at me, exposing my presence obviously. Still, I searched diligently to no avail. Ramses stall still stood empty. *'Where was my wonderful Ramses? Where had Lucas taken him? And if not Lucas then who had taken him?'* The sheriff had found no sign of the animal's hoof prints leading away from the plantation, other than those easily accounted for.

The cemetery, the glade on the knoll, all brought fruitless results. I now stood by the well on the top of the hill to the west of the mansion. *'Why dig a well on the top of a hill?'* Most people dig a well on low ground, hoping to his water sooner with less work involved. Jefferson had shown me the well and the well house close by. The well house was a plain, framed affair not in keeping with the rest of the estate. There was only a board floor, and four walls holding a minimum of tools and clay pipe. There wasn't even a loft. The roof timbers lay exposed. A few ropes and chains hung from them. Back into the lowering sunlight I trod slowly. *'Why such a plain building?'*

The well was another matter, entirely. It was very large, at least six feet across the opening. The sides were of a quarried stone, large ones weighing many tons. The gray granite blocks and slabs interlocked very closely together. Each would probably have to be set in place by a block and tackle. No mere man could have lifted them. The sides were high, also. *'Why?'*

Over the hole was a round wooden top like the roof of a gazebo. It was built of very, heavy, oaken beams. At the center of which was the water gears and lifts with no need for rope and bucket. Jefferson had explained that a special engineer had travelled all the way from Spain to build this remarkable contraption. It was said that the secret of this water lift lay in the aged archaeology of Egypt. The engineer had traveled around the world, seeking the knowledge of Pharaohs and the latest inventors of Venice and elsewhere.

The top was an ingenious giant pulley over which a thick cable ran. This drove a pipe-like gear with extensions at the end of which, large buckets, or bowls of steel were affixed. The buckets could be turned upward, due to a hinged connection. They could not turn downward. Around the outside rim of the well was a round bowl-like cistern which went all the way around. One part of this was lower than the rest, ending in a dark drain pipe.

As the buckets arrived at the top, they would tilt over, thus dumping their cargo into the rim's cistern. The water travelled down the hill to the old mansion and the garden fountain was also supplied. The whole thing depended on a strong mule or horse to travel around and around the old well. A steel pipe went from the top of the well's roof about twelve feet, at its end, of which was a chain and a collar hanging down. This enormous circle being plodded by the animal turned the gear faster, thus, raising a steady supply of water in quite large amounts.

Absolutely no one was ever allowed down the well which understandable at the very least. Jefferson told me of a young Negro boy who had broken this rule and climbed down inside using the extended buckets like a ladder. There was a bench near where this hapless individual had probably sat in the hot sun. The mule was driven by a strong arm and a long switch. After the cisterns at the house and barns were full, the mule was to be unhitched and turned out to pasture

On this day, however, the boy had probably been very hot, sitting in the sun. He had decided to climb down into the well, leaving the mule standing patiently waiting to be unhitched. He would satisfy his curiosity as well as, enjoy a quick cool off. The temperature inside the roofed, shaded, well must have been very inviting. Soon after the boy climbed over the high stone wall, something tragic happened, a pesky, horsefly perhaps, or something else began to irritate the mule. The mule promptly tried to end the torment by running away from it.

"Ol J.C.," Jefferson said, "would allow no one but himself to climb down inside the well to retrieve the body. He sho' was mad, the Colonel was! He had the boys friend hoss whipped foah leavin' him alone on tha job!" A sign was put up warning of, "Danger", "No Trespassing!", "Keep Away!"

Some said the Colonel used a ships spyglass to keep watch on the well. Anyone caught within a certain radius of the well was horse whipped. Only certain trusted ones were authorized to approach the well until they were of a certain age. Then the Colonel took them down inside the well to satisfy their curiosity and to explain its workings. Only one had broken the rule before the agreed time, and that was Lucas. "T'was ah terrible beaten he got den. Ol Colonel was fit to be tied! Aftah the beaten, he taken Lucas up to his room and you could heah low talkin mostly murmurin." Nobody dayhud tah' evesdrop on thet mawnin, no Suh!"

I stood on a bucket to look down inside the old well. The arms of the huge dippers went down, down, into the blackness. The water level could not be seen. The walls were cut stone that also disappeared into the blackness. I felt a strong urge to climb down into the cold, damp interior.

"Oh, it was perfectly safe," I decided. The pulley chain hung still and impotent. "I'll be very careful," Promising myself as I climbed atop the wall and placed a foot on the top dipper. It was solid. No problem. There, I allowed my weight to slowly come to bear on the arm. Then the other foot, I grasped the arm. Then the other foot, I grasped the arms above me and gazed apprehensively downward. I could see no bottom!

"What was it Jefferson had said? Dat ol' well, she so deep, some addled folks round heah thinks she goes way down to whe'ah de bad spirits stays! Mebe down to de debbil!" I stopped!

'Kelly, ol girl, you are not as daring as you once were. What are you waiting for?' I descended slowly, deliberately, being very careful to test each step and arm in turn. I had descended for a good distance when I hear a noise. It sounded like chain rattling, perhaps the chain on the pulley arm. All at

once, I was frightened. *'What could be happening? Kelly, your imagination is playing tricks on you. "* The chain rattled again softly. "Only a gentle puff of wind," I reasoned. "Only the wind." I turned my gaze to the wall of the old well. It was then that I saw it. A niche in the wall of the well, wooden torches lay within. *"Why? To see with of course, but to see what, the bottom of the well perhaps? '*

It was darker down here. I reached out to take one of the torches. It was dry and had been soaked in kerosene at one time. I stuck the torch into the waistband of my blouse. One lowered step, then two, before I thought of fire. *'How to light the torch, maybe there was flint and steel'...*

I started to climb back up to inspect the niche farther than the gear of the well turned very slowly. I watched in shock as it began to pick up speed.

"How, oh, my.... help!" I screamed. "Stop, stop the well! I'm down here!" I shrieked..."Help!" Then I noticed the machinery was turning the wrong way. Instead of bringing water up to the top of the well, it was taking me ever downward, toward the water. There would be no chance for surviving or holding on after the buckets hit the water's surface. I would be driven and beaten under by the ever increasing, ever turning of the arms. Already it was turning quicker, my footing on the arm was getting more and more precarious. I screamed again.

"Oh, HELP! For GOD'S SAKE please, PLEASE STOP!" I could see the glint of water now, as I was down perhaps two or three hundred feet. I watched, saving my breath for the water. Whoever was on top obviously could not hear me or did not care! This time, whoever it was stood a very good chance of getting the job done. The water came closer and closer. *'Way down there,'* I stared with horror. *'Way down there you will never be found! Way down there in this cold dark well.'*

The water was close now. I could feel and smell it as the paddle arms entered on one side and came back up on the other. I prayed fervently, "Oh, Lord please......."

16

~The Secret~

The splashing of the bucket arms grew louder. I could see no hope, no escape. Closer and closer drew what most certainly would be my demise. *'Oh, what to do?'*

"Help! Lucas!" *'Now why did I call his name?'*

"Kelly, my darling, tis the final bow you'll be taking," my father's voice haunted me! His apparition appeared before me, and then his likeness was replaced in the water's spray.

"The Colonel!" With a long, bony finger, the spirit pointed,

"Loooo-oo-k well-ll!" The banshee's voice echoed hollowly inside the old well, "Loo-k w-ell-ll!" The finger pointed, and I looked! *'There! There only a turn or two from the water I saw it. A dark opening! In the well's wall, a tunnel!'*

It was almost impossible to keep my balance on the wet metal arm. One foot slipped, then another. Fortunately, I had strong arms! *'Here it comes!'* I would only get one chance, one chance, mistress of Claibourne, one chance to throw myself into the dark mouth of that oh-so-small tunnel. My leap must be perfect, or the arm above would surely strike me, driving me into the water.

"Oh, Father in heaven"... I leaped!

The upper part of my body struck the muddy earth of the tunnels right side. I was almost in, but I was slipping, slipping! Then my muddy fingers grasped stone! A stone walkway! I dug into the joints between the stones. I felt the rip of my fingernails. Now! I drove forward. *'Hurry!'*

The blow struck me in the calf area of my leg, a raking, bruising, lacerating wound tore the skin and flesh, ending by sliding from the bone of my left ankle. The pain was devastating. I felt quite dizzy. *But I was safe! 'Failed again, they had failed again!'* Oh I could have shouted and laughed in their face! I almost did. But cold reason instructed me. *'Keep quiet! Do you want them to know? If they come after you, you shall be unable to flee! They cannot fail then!'*

I leaned against the muddy wall of the tunnel. The clammy dampness penetrated the material of my clothing. I was sitting on the stone pathway, no, a stand up tunnel this! I, however, could only move by bending over, in my case I should have to crawl, but only after my trembling and dizziness passed. *'Oh, the pain! The terrible, excruciating pain!'*

In the dim light from the well I could see the wound was bleeding! I tore my short, half petty coat into bandages after cleaning my hands as much as possible with my jacket. My poor hands were also sore and bleeding. I wrapped my leg from knee to ankle. The swelling had already begun! I dared not remove my riding boot, for I should not be able to get it back on again. *'Where did this tunnel lead?'* Perhaps it was a dead end. If it was I was still a goner, for sure. I could not climb back up the well's machinery. The arms were still turning and splashing.

I reached for the wooden torch, and I removed it from my waist band. *'If I could not light it, I could use it as a club!'* As I grasped the club it struck metal that sounded hollow.

"A box... a box, of what?" I felt into the darkness for the box of tin. The lid lifted rustily. Inside there was ....
'a flint and steel!' There were more torches there also! And

tinder, tinder for fire! But I dare not light a fire! Whoever must be at the top of the well would surely be listening and watching, watching for any signs of life and that I still live! I sat and waited, shivering in the cold draft of the tunnel.

At last, the old well was slowing down! With a clack and a rusty squeal, the arms swung slowly to a stop! *'Now! Now, they would surely be listening, and looking, looking down the well! Waiting or a weak cry, or a splash, I must be very still!'* Minutes passed that seemed like hours.

'Was it safe yet? Had they gone? I must wait, wait!' A long while later, the clank of the chain pull sounded. They were not so careful now! They believed me dead, and unable to hear their carelessness. *'Oh, the blaggard, or blaggard's, whatever, I must wait until I knew they were gone!'* My little pistol was still in my jacket. I gloated and pictured in my mind their surprise. *'I shall show no mercy.'*

But now the light was almost gone. *'I must try again.'* Opening the box, I removed the flint and steel, praying that the box had been dry inside. I placed the tinder well inside the opening. Shielding the light as much as possible with my body, pain from my hands almost made me cry out as the steel struck the flint.

'There! Again!' Time after time sparks flew, but they did not catch the tinder. Even with sound hands, this would be hard. Now it was harder still.

'Oh please!" Yes! A spark! A glow! *Blow gently, care-ful-ly! Smoke!'* The little tendril curled upward, and then turned into a small flame. I quickly wrapped some old rags around the kerosene torch and lit them. I put my pistol in my waistband, and kicked out the tinder's last flame. My torched blazed forth into the darkness of the tunnel.

"I hoped that it is not too far," I begged, "Please don't let it be too far." I began my torturous journey into the debts of the tunnel on hands and knees, or on one hand, at least. The other clutched my torch. "Oh please, let there be no snakes!"

The tunnel made a slight bend.

"What was around the corner?" I felt for my pistol. It was still there, its weight reassuring. My fears were unfounded; there was only this one tunnel! Slowly, slowly, slowly, painfully, I crawled... Now my knee struck an up turned stone,

"Oww!" No more please! The tunnel turned upward. *'Stairs! Stone stairs! Could I make it?'* My torch wouldn't last forever. I must try! Upward, upward! At the top of the stairs the tunnel became wider, higher, one could walk upright now. A lot of good that did me, I must still crawl along, slowly. Oh, so slowly! I could see a stone doorway ahead. *'What would be there? Who would be there? What was that? Voices! Faint, oh so faint! A voice! Oh, if they should see my light!'* Oh how I hated to do it! I dreaded the darkness that should prevail as soon as the torch was extinguished! I must travel the last few yards in darkness; there was no hope for it!

Just as soon as I put out the light, terror gripped my soul. Blackness like no other smothered my very breath. I tried to hurry. *'This will not do, Kelly, old girl,'* My father *laughing and smilingly teased, 'T'will not do a'tall, you're too much a tomboy, I wager.'*

He was right, I must go slower, be much more careful. There, I was inside the doorway of a small room. Through a square light in the ceiling, I could see a ladder leading upward. There was a trap door standing open. Lamplight glowed faintly. I crawled to the bottom of the ladder and looked upward. I grasped my little revolver, pointed it at the square opening. I listened,

"So! So many times you've tried. And now, now my little Yankee, my little mistress of Claibourne, is finally dead!"

'"Lucas!" There was no doubt! *It was his voice, up there gloating that I was dead! His voice!'* Starting down low then rising with anger as he cried again.

"My little Yankee is dead!" There was a shuffle, the thud of running footsteps and he, he who had shouted gleefully at my death leaped through the opening of the trap door, landing a sprawl in front of me! He grabbed the ladder to stand himself up on his feet. I rose to my knees, fury and heartbreak made my voice shrill.

"I'm not dead yet, you cur!" His eyes, those black eyes widened with surprise. He moved toward me.

"Kelly!" I ... I fired twice! Thrice, I fired. My anger did not help my aim, for the little gun waivered and shook. But Lucas Claibourne, my, *'would be',* murderer, was dead! He fell violently against the wall. I slowly came to myself. I threw the little gun into the corner. Suddenly, the enormity of what I had done possessed me. The last thing I saw as I passed out was the face of Judge Hansen grinning down at me from the trap door. Behind him, I could see the face of Dawkins, the old overseer, rotten teeth glinting terribly. The judge had a gun in his hand, as did Dawkins.

"I'm sorry, I had to... I murmured to the judge... "I had to..." And I could see no more. I fainted.

17

~Suspicions~

I came to, only to see the body of Lucas Claibourne still lying where he had fallen. The Judge and Dawkins were talking animatedly.

"Couldn't have turned out no better," The judge crowed, pushing back his spectacles.

"Yeah," Dawkins put in with a wolfish grin.

"Stead o' us hevin' tuh kill ol' Lucas, she done it fer us, haw, haw! An' he was ready to die fer her, he was! He took a chance he did, knowin' we both had him covered. He lammed me one, he did! Thet cane o' his hurt some, I tells ye! I seen stars! He'd escaped, sho' nuff if'n she hadn't shot him! Haw! Haw!"

"We'll do the same as we done all them other times." Dawkins put in. "We'll leave his boot tracks and cane prints all over the place. Folks'll think she killed him in self defense a'fore she died. An' jes' in case, we'll lock the trap door, and put the feed bin back over h'it, nobody will be the wiser."

"No!" Judge Hansen put in, "I want em found. Thet way, there won't be any problem in getting the place back! We got rid o'her brother and she's got no other kin. I'll pick up the place for practically nuthin', now! No thanks to you, you gamblin' fool! I ought a stop your clock fer what you done, losin' tha place at gambling!"

"Now judge, I didn't mean tuh.... They's no harm

done, now, ye got'er back, lock, stock, and barrel, haint ye?" From the way Dawkins was cowering, you could see the fear that he had for the judge. The banker was by far the most dangerous man.

"An' remember, Judge, ye couldn't a' done 'er without me an' tha' missus' help! Sho an' didn't she play Missy June real good, haw, haw! Sent chills up my backbone, even, she did!"

"Don't take much to scare a coward," the judge growled. "They aint got no backbone!"

"No call fer thet kinda talk," whined Dawkins.

"We've jawed 'round enough!" Banker Hansen growled again, "Time to hit tha road! No! Leave her gun! If they don't find a gun, they'll know somebody else was here!" He moved closer to peer directly down at me. I held my breath. He kicked my wounded leg. It shot pain all the way up my spine.

'*Don't move, Kelly old girl, if you want to live!*' Somehow, I still held my breath, and made no sound. The judge held his spectacles before my mouth and nose. Then he straightened and turned to Dawkins.

"No breath!" She's dead, I reckon."

"Ain't ye gonna check him?" Dawkins queried.

"Nah, no need, she fired three shots. An' one musta' got him in tha' head, look'it all thet blood!" He turned,

"Thanks ah' heap missy, you sho hev' helped us a lot, heh, heh! "Let's go!" I heard them climb the ladder.

"Leave the trap door open!" the judge ordered. I heard a sound like a kick, and ... then the rattle of a padlock. "Thet does it! Guess they will find 'em in a little while!

"Sure they will, sooner or later, heh, heh, heh!"

All was dark again. I could smell the kerosene of the torch where I had set it against the wall. I had nothing to light it again. I crawled toward Lucas. *'Oh, my Lord help me, I have shot an innocent man! I have killed the man that I loved, who had loved me! He hadn't killed Franklin!'* I felt of his body, searching for a pulse.

'Yes!' It was faint, but regular. His breath was even, steady. *'Lucas was alive!'* With bloody fingers I examined the head wound. There was a deep furrow, but the bullet had not entered the skull. I could find no other wounds on him. But the head wound was still dangerous. He might have a severe concussion, or even a skull fracture. He could still die! I prayed fervently, and then I cleaned and dressed the wound in the dark. He started to moan. I took him in my arms and held him. I kissed the unruly lock of hair that he was always brushing away from his forehead.

"Oh, my love, you wanted to save me! And I shot you! Oh, heaven forgive me!" Lucas's body seemed to relax. I cried now, heartbroken sobs that jerked my body in spasms.

"I've killed you! Daddy said that my temper would be the death of me, but it's turned out to be your death. Oh, I love you, I love you, I love you! Oh, I am so sorry, my darling, so sorry!"

"Ah am too, sorry, ma'am." The poor dead lips whispered. "Ah am too sorry, foah if ah'm truly dead, ah couldn't do this!" My sobs caught in my throat as the sweet lips pressed weakly to mine.

"My darling!" I covered his face with my tearful kisses. "Please, please, forgive me, I didn't know...."

"Shush darlin," Lucas whispered, "Ah have been shot befoah! Ah'm not dead yet. Whea did tha lowdown Judge and Dawkins go? Ah' got to do something!" He tried to rise.

"No! Lucas! NO! You must wait a while!" He fell back into my arms breathing heavily.

"Ah guess so, sho nuff, foah ah'm awful weak right

now." I held him while he slept. Soon, the sound of morning drifted down into my consciousness. I heard the horses neighing to be fed. I could hear birds. There was no used trying to climb the trap door. Apparently Jefferson had not returned yet. Should I wait? Lucas needed medical attention. No, I must try; try to find a way out of here. It could mean the difference between life and death for Lucas.

I searched around the little room, but found nothing. I went to the stone doorway. There was a stone landing, and then the stairs. I started slowly down. My leg was still swollen and throbbed incessantly. I made it to the bottom step after careful negotiating and then I had to sit down to rest.

After a while, my eyes began to adjust to the dimness and I could see the stairs built against the high stone foundations of the room above. The room was underground of course. *'What was it that Dawkins had said? The trapdoor usually been hidden by the feed bin?'* The room alone and this tunnel must have been kept a secret from everyone. I knew now why the Colonel had refused to allow anyone near the well. It was not just the danger, for he had wanted to keep this tunnel and the room under the tack room floor a secret, *'but why all this secrecy?'* All that I could see was just a room and a tunnel. Both were empty. Suddenly I got goose bumps. Perhaps they were not so empty at all. I remembered the Colonel's ghost pointing and saying,

"Look Well!" But he was showing me the tunnel to save my life, wasn't he? Then I remembered the first time. He had said something. I had not been in the well at that time. He must mean to say,

'Look in the well!" "Look well!" Something I was sure, gave the words meaning. *'Someday, if I ever got out of here alive, I must go back, back up the steps.'*

Lucas still lay sleeping deeply. I needed sleep also, for

I had held him all night. Now I was very tired. So tired! I cuddled close to his warm body. Oh I just had to rest, to get a little rest. *'Just a short nap, and then I'll find a way out if I have to climb that old well pump again,* ' If my injured leg would let me...

I was having a nightmare. I couldn't breathe! Something or someone held me imprisoned. I could not move! Then that someone put his lips to my ear and said,

"Shhhhh, Kelly, foah heaven's sake be still an' doan' cry out! Someone's a'commin', yo'heah, shake yo' head if yo understand'?"

I shook my head affirmative. Lucas removed his hand from my mouth. For the first time, I realized that the good air had a taste, a wonderful life giving taste as delicious as cool water. I drank deeply. Lucas held me close, very close. Was this really necessary? I didn't hear anything. I listened.

'Hoof beats, horses, a lot of them, but what if it is Hansen?' I remembered my little revolver. There were still three shots left. Enough for the pair of them, the scoundrels! Then the hoof beats were close, very close! They stopped, and I heard voices! But they too quieted and I couldn't hear anything intelligible.

Hansen and Dawkins! It had to be! No one else knew where we were! My suspicions were confirmed as I heard the thump, thump of boot feet upon the tack room floor! Now they were to the trap door. There was movement above the opening! Lucas released to crouch, tense and ready to spring upon the intruder. He waivered and put a hand to his head dizzily. Then he steadied. I pulled the gun from my pocket.

"No, my darling, you should not have to fight in your condition." I decided grimly. "This time, I shall hold steady, I shall not miss."

A leg was lowered through the trap door. A booted foot

sought the top rung of the ladder. Then two, three steps downward, Jefferson! It was Jefferson! Oh, thank you, heaven....

"Yo', boss, are yo' down heah?" His low, gentle voice queried. Then in the trap doors opening there appeared a heavy face. *'Hansen!'* I quickly raised the gun to fire. Hansen was there in the dark above Jefferson! I centered the sights on that hated face and my finger tightened!

18

~Salvation~

"Look out, boss!" yelled Jefferson! Lucas struck my arm spoiling my aim. The shot went wild into the ceiling. I heard a cry, and then a deep voice demanded.

"Throw down thet gun, you triggah happy fools! Throw it down, I say. If'n yo' don't theah's five armed men, t'will fill thet hole full o'lead!"

"Its awl' right mistuh sherrif," Jefferson gaffawed. "Hit wuz just mah mistress a goin' off half-cocked, sho an she still ah fire-eaten one, hain' she, boss!" Jefferson's smile was returned by Lucas. He had taken my gun.

"Sho nuff is! But ah'm awful glad thet she is! Ah might hev froze tuh death if'n it' had not been foah her warm nature!" I blushed furiously. *'Oh, he was a taunting one, wasn't he!'*

Jefferson and one of the sheriff's deputies helped Lucas through the hole. They had wanted me to go first, but I insisted that Lucas go first. Why did they carry on so! Any fool could see that Lucas was wounded!

"Sho, an' aint she ah red-headed wonder!" said Lucas. The sheriff growled,

"Hain' she tho, she also lak' tuh blowed muh head off if'n ya'll hadn't taken that little gun!"

"Watch the leg!" I angrily demanded.

"Go easy theah, boys," Lucas soothed. "she ain' been trained yet. Ah reckon ah'm gonna hev mah hands full teachin' her to be ah lady, ah reckon! Sho now, an' ah always loved ah filly with spirit!"

"Oh! Who do you think you are talking to, you, you, rebel!" I shot back.

"To mah dahlin wife and lovah, an sweetheart, and ever' thin' else that is deah an' precious in tha world, dahlin'. Ah'm askin you all to marry me, ma'am, if'n yo will excuse me bein' ah poor cripple." The black eyes warmed and glowed at me with genuine seriousness. I was dumbstruck.

"Lucas!" I said softly.

"Yes, dahlin?"

"You're teasing me again, aren't you? Being sarcastic?" I had a strange urge to laugh and cry at the same time.

"Sho am not!" Lucas reached for me. Shamelessly I fell into his arms. A whoop from Jefferson echoed into the night as my future husband held me close and guided me on the way to the house.

"We gonna have a sho' nuff southuhn weddin' right heah at Claibourne, yippee!"

"And ah Yankee one!" I rejoined with a laugh!

The hot, steaming coffee tasted and felt wonderful. After a while, the sheriff began to question Lucas and I about the last twenty four hour ordeal. Alex Robbins had prepared the coffee, and he sat awestruck, as did Lucas while I told of the harrowing descent into the well. I discretely left out the part about the Colonel's ghost. Lucas's black-eyes shot fire at the telling.

"Ah'll kill thet banker!"

"K'aint!" Sheriff Abrams returned. "He's already daid!" It was our turn to stare as the sheriff turned the floor over to Alex. Alex's lawyer self took over as the story unfolded.

"First of all, our firm, eh, has been doing an investigation, eh, query into the dealings of said Judge. He's no judge, at all, so Banker Hansen, or should I say, Mr. Mortimer Johns! Mr. Johns is his true name. He fled to the south some years ago. The patrons of the bank that he was the president of soon discovered some quite shady deals that Mr. Johns had perpetrated. Actually, it was one of the bank clerks who discovered the shortages. The poor fellow paid with his life for his honesty. Mr. Johns was discovered missing along with the total assets of the bank. No one knew where he had gone until he started the same little operation here in Columbia."

"We knew this Hansen, was shady, but we could not prove anything until we had Dawkins confession. Just as he did with the "bogus" deed from Claibourne plantation, Dawkins lost heavily at gambling. He thought to recover his losses by wagering your horse, Miss Rhyman. But as the first time, he lost the horse, and I just happened to be acquainted with the gentlemen that won Ramses. In fact, I was the one who set up the game, ha, ha, ha! I always suspected Mr. Johns was behind the attempts on Kel-er, Miss Rhyman's life, so I arranged for a little pressure to be put on his weak henchman, Dawkins."

"Mr. Johns and Dawkins conspired to retrieve Claibourne Manor the same way they had acquired it the first time, by getting *'rid'* of the legal owners."

"So they murdered my father!" Lucas.

"Yes, and faked the will that left the estate to Dawkins."

"So the deed, the deed that my father won is worthless?" I felt quite helpless as I realized that my Claibourne, or perhaps even Lucas Claibourne, might be lost to me.

125

"Yes, Miss Rhyman, the deed is worthless. But the true deed was never found by Dawkins or Mr. Johns, 'Hansen', as we knew him. Also, there were certain-er-valuables, that were missing, namely your mother's jewelry among other items. They just simply disappeared. Both Dawkins and Hansen believed the other stolen them and pulled a double-cross on the other."

"What is to become of the estate?" I questioned.

"It will be held in court until the original geed is found. If after one year, the deed has not been found the estate will fall to whoever has paid the back taxes for the place. That would be you, Miss Rhyman." Lucas looked crest fallen.

"To me and my husband Mr. Robbins," I looked at Lucas, "to me and my husband!" Lucas stared at me unsmilingly. He turned to speak to the sheriff.

"Yo say thet Hansen is dead? What about Mr. Dawkins?" Sheriff Abrams looked at Lucas levelly.

"He is dead, too! Tried tuh grab one o' my guns whilest ah was shootin' it out with this Mortimer feller. Gun went off, and Dawkin's wuz gut shot. He signed ah death confession."

The sheriff took his leave, along with his deputies and Alex. I thanked Alex profusely for his help and determined that he would be rewarded handsomely for his faithful and life-saving efforts. Lucas was very quiet. I sat down beside him before the fireplace.

"I am so sorry about your father, Lucas."

"And ah'm sorry about youah brothah, dahlin. Yo' know thet ah'm innocent of doin him hahm, doan yo?"

"Oh yes, darling, I beg your forgiveness for thinking such a thing. Oh, I had hoped it wasn't you, oh heavens," I broke into sobs. "Oh, please, please forgive me. I love you so much." Lucas pulled me into his arms.

126

"Sho, dahlin' yo is forgiven from my heart, which belongs to you. But ah yo' shuah dahlin?"

"What?" I tearfully gazed into his eyes. "Thet you will marry me know'in what people will say."

"Say what?" I asked softly, fearfully. Was Lucas changing his mind?

"Ah, they mos' probably will say thet I married you jest to get Claibourne back." Lucas's black eyes clouded. "But if'n ya'all is still willin' we'll suffah it, if'n yo' doin' believe that it's so? Ah couldn't marry you if you thought it was so!"

"Oh fiddlesticks," I flared. "I'm marrying you, no buts about it!" Lucas's eyes glowed with fire. "Besides," I added.

"Besides what, dahlin?"

"Besides, I've got some husband training to do! And I always like my hosses to have fire!" I said sweetly. Lucas grinned, his white teeth flashing.

"Be cay-ah full bout playin' with fiah, dahlin, you might get burned!" He wasn't bluffing! The fire of our embrace left me breathless.

"Lucas, darling," I murmured, "sweetheart!" Lucas's low voice answered,

"Yes, dahlin?"

"I ah, think that I, ah, know where your fathers will is hidden, maybe?" Lucas was visibly struck.

"Yo have it, Kelly? Sho' an' yo wouldn't have..."

"No darling, I don't have it. But I think, ah, your father the Colonel, he told me where it is... Maybe...." I lamely quipped. Then I recounted to Lucas the details of his father's ghost pointing and saying, *'Look well.'*

"I believe he was telling me to look in the well," I gravely stated. Lucas visibly shivered as he gazed up at the fiery old Colonel's portrait.

"Ah yo' sho' yo' didn't imagine, ah, perhaps yo' wuz delirious or something, dahlin?" I shook my head.

"No, Lucas, he pointed, and I heard him."

After Lucas and I recovered from our aches and pains, we decided to go ahead and arrange for the wedding. I sent out the invitations. Everything was wonderful, except for Lucas. He came from town cold and silent. When I asked him what was wrong he looked away and said,

"Nuthin's wrong!" Then he stalked out to the barns. That's where he spent most of his time, now.

Jefferson soon confided to me as to the cause of Lucas's behavior and state of mind. Someone in town, in a drunken stupor, had blurted out a joke about a rich carpetbagger lady and a poor plantation owner. The inference was obvious! Lucas was marrying me for my money. The wedding was only one week off. I had to try to put the rumors to rest.

"Colonel, if you can hear me, oh, please, guide us to where your will is hidden. And, if you please, by doing so give me your blessing to marry your son!" We searched the tunnel thoroughly and found nothing. Lucas's father was quite a no-show during this endeavor.

"Thet does it, ah guess," Lucas dejectedly slapped his hand against his leg.

"No it doesn't," I adamantly replied. "Your father said, "Look well!" and that's where I'm going next!"

"Sho an' yo' are not!" Lucas flared, "if yo think thet ah'm goin' tuh allow yo to climb back down into thet ol' well yo sho' aiah crazy. No, mah dahlin..." he added to take the sting off his rebuke. I looked at him.

"But we'll do it different this time, sweetheart, we'll tie ropes around us and Jefferson can stand guard at the top. So you see it will be perfectly safe." Lucas looked doubtful.

128

Lucas let the way down into the damp interior of the well. Jefferson watched apprehensively at the top He paid out the rope little by little, passing it around the top of one of the heavy oaken beams. If we fell we would be brought up short with no harm incurred. Or so we hoped! Slowly, we traversed each step in turn, stopping at each to observe and investigate the stone wall of the old well and even the steel of the machinery.

As we got deeper, I began to feel apprehension. I remembered my ordeal from before. So far, nothing! Deeper, and deeper, step by step, now we were almost at the bottom when the hair on the back of my neck began to prickle. I clutched at Lucas. He looked at me quizzickly. I whispered to him,

"Here, don't you feel that, something's about to happen!" Lucas whispered back.

"Sho an' yo' doin reckon..." His eyes began to reflect a green luminescent light. I followed Lucas's gaze. Colonel Jasper Calhoun Claibourne pointed his ghostly finger directly at the stone wall of the well.

"Looo-oook wel-ll!" He turned his head and looked directly at Lucas and I sternly. I could feel Lucas tremble. Then the apparition of Lucas's father smiled!

"Thank you, Colonel," I whispered. His body slowly faded until only his hand and bony finger was still pointing at the wall, then it too was gone.

"Oh my lawd Kelly, thet wuz my fathuh foah sho, did yo see him honey?"

"Yes, I sure did. Somehow, I'm not scared of him anymore.

"An' did yo' see him smile? Sho' an' ah nevuh seen him smile like thet since befo'ah muthah died! He used to smile all the time then, 'cause mothuh wuz still alive. He foah sho

129

loved huh, Fathuh did. He jus' wasn't the same aftah she passed away." I touched his arm.

"I have a feeling that he is happy again with her."

"Oh, thet sho would be wonderful," Lucas breathed.

As soon as we regained our composure, we moved downward. Down, down, to the place where the Colonel had appeared.

"Look, Lucas! There, that stone! There above the water! That's where he pointed!"

"Sho an' if thet's not the lettah "C" chipped out in it, or am ah goin' blind?" Lucas excitedly answered. Southerners usually spoke slow, unless excited about something. Lucas was talking almost as fast as I was, now. He had a small bag of tools around his neck. He reached inside to remove a chisel and hammer.

"Sho now, hold onto mah belt at the back, dahlin." I grabbed his belt while holding onto one of the arms of the spiral gear.

'Clang,' then the hammer and chisel was put away and a small pry bar was inserted into the joints of the stone. You could clearly read the letter, 'C' chiseled into its face, Claibourne!

"Heah, Dahlin, hold fast," Lucas panted. "Heah, befoah ah take the stone out any farthuh we'll tie one of these ropes around it."

"Ah don't want it to fall down to tha' bottom of tha' well," he wheezed. "Now tie the othuh end around thet arm theh! Now look out! Ahm goin to take this ol rock out all the way!" A crunch, a grind, the smell of sparks, and the stone fell free! It swung dangerously for a moment, and then it hung heavily, secured to the metal arm.

"Oh dahlin"... breathed Lucas.

"What! What do you see? Tell me Lucas!" Lucas said

wistfully,

"Ah see mothuh's jewelry box! An, an, anothuh box! An' anuthuh! Fathuh sho nuff kept the cahpet baggahs from gettin' anythin'!" Lucas grinned joyfully.

"Oh! Wonderful! Oh Lucas, do you know what this means... that Claibourne belongs to you and has all the time! And all those biddies who've been talking will have to eat their words!"

"But how ah' they goin to know, dahlin?"

"Oh they'll know, when you sho the deed to the people in the land office, and the tax office!" "Oh I'm so happy that I could just die! But I can't die for a long time now!" Lucas bit directly into the bait that I dangled in front of him.

"Why dahlin, why can't yo die for ah long time, now?"

"Cause," I teased, "I've got a husband to train!" "And it's going to be a long, hot job!" Lucas grinned.

"The fire, I mean" Lucas's eyes flushed.

"Heah, yo' sho; is askin to get kissed!"

"Well if you have to fight fire, the best place to do it is in a well. Where there is water you know, if you're crazy enough to use it. It's such a sweet fire one cannot find the will to extinguish such a sweet throbbing pain." "Do you want to go inside?" Lucas queried breathlessly after we were safe out of the well. Our eyes met. I could feel the fire leap stronger in my blood as I gazed into my sweethearts eyes.

"No, let's go to the oak glade, our glade." I smiled.

Hours later, as we lay on a blanket beneath the oaks I played with the unruly curl on Lucas's forehead. He lay contently with his head on a cool green bed of moss. A strange, solemn sound broke the silence.

"OOOOOOO, OOOOOOH, OOOOOOOH, AHHHH, OHHHHH, OOOH, OOHH!" *There it was again! That sound!*

"Lucas dearest, please do tell me what is that sound! It sounds so, so utterly lonesome and forlorn."

"Sho dahlin, when yo heahs that sound, sho' an you know that yo is sho nuff in tha' South. Foah that is a moanin' dove."

"Oh is it hurt?" I asked him. He laughed.

"No dahlin, he's callin' for his mate, who is lost or maybe dead. Doves mate foah life, you know." He gently added. "An' theah's ah legend that the reason that he is ah' moanin', he is missin' an' pinin' ovah his sweetheart. Doves migrate to the no'ath in tha' summah an' come back south in tha' wintah."

"They say that the maon'in dove is tha' spirit of ah confederate soljah cryin' out foah his lost love! An' they say it's true because tha' dove is all dressed in gray, an his feet are all stained with blood from tha' battlefields. An' on his breast is tha' rose of tha suthun' sunrise, sho nuff' now!" Lucas' eyes took on a haunted, tormented look.

"A lot o' us suthun' boys went noath, but some o' us didn't come back. An' a lot o' those that did, ayah' still pinin' ovuh they-uh lost loved ones. Me an' a lot o' them will nevah see theah sweethearts again." He dropped his eyes. "Ah can't nevah hear that sound without wantin' to cry." The sound came again, mournful and plaintively pleading, *'come, come, comin', home, --com-in' home.'* I cradled Lucas' head to my breast.

"Oh, Lucas, darling, you're home at last, home to stay. And I promise you, your home and your sweetheart are yours forever, if you'll have me?" I wept unashamedly as I kissed the poor quivering lips. Lucas's eyes were shut, but I could see the tracks of tears starting to slide down his cheeks.

"Sho', dahlin, an' ah' reckon that this moawnin' dove got no need to call no mo'..."

~About Jim Wade Smith~

~~~

Jim Wade Smith, was born and raised from childhood in the Appalachian, (pronounced: app ah lay chan) mountains of North Carolina. Growing up under Mount Mitchell and near Grandfather Mountain, the family was poor and lived in a shack built of sawmill planks.

A Diphtheria survivor, Jim, at the age of four,

miraculously survived the old county doctor's, "Kill or Cure shot." This was actual words the doctor used for the description of the medicine that he administered. At the time there was no cure for the illness and the medicine was a long shot whether it would help him recover.

Over the years of his life Jim played sports such as bowling, tennis, fishing and baseball. He played minor league baseball so well that he garnered a contract offer for the Brooklyn Dodgers but being only 19, he was too young to sign the contract. He had to be 21 years of age. His father refused to sign, stating,

"I need you here, boy." His father was illiterate and could not read the contract himself.

Jim has written occasionally over his life time. He is the author and illustrator of his own comic series called, 'Ol Cavey', written and drawn while he was working third shift as a security guard was a hit with his family and co workers. One western novel he wrote, and entered into the Louis L'amour book competition placed but the book wasn't ever published. This novel, 'Call of the Dove', was written in the 1990's and again however, he had not seriously perused getting it published until now.

At the young age of 74, Jim is a retired brick mason. He still is a dead eye deer hunter. You can find him often, studying his King James Bible, just beginning to write up his own mountain short stories and excerpts, as well as having read most of the books in the local library. He is an ordained licensed minister, married to his wife Trina McKinney Smith, grandfather and now a great granddad!

The history of America is also one of his passions. Someone asked him what did he pray for the most? With tear filled, gentle, caring eyes he answered,

"The little children of the world"

~~~

Jim Wade Smith

~~~